Confessions of a Poisoner,
Written by Herself

T0306755

Texts and Translations

Members of the series board who approved publication of this volume: Joseph R. Allen, Muhsin J. al-Musawi, Rosemary Arrojo, Daniel Balderson, Michael Henry Heim, Janis A. Mayes, and Lawrence Venuti (chair)

The Texts and Translations series was founded in 1991 to provide students and teachers with important texts not readily available or not available at an affordable price and in high-quality translations. The books in the series are intended for students in upper-level undergraduate and graduate courses in national literatures in languages other than English, comparative literature, ethnic studies, area studies, translation studies, women's studies, and gender studies. The Texts and Translations series is overseen by an editorial board composed of specialists in several national literatures and in translation studies.

For a complete listing of titles, see the last pages of this book.

Confessions of a Poisoner, Written by Herself

Translated and introduced by
Raleigh Whitinger and Diana Spokiene

The Modern Language Association of America
New York 2009

©2009 by The Modern Language Association of America
All rights reserved
Printed in the United States of America

MLA and MODERN LANGUAGE ASSOCIATION are trademarks owned by the Modern Language Association of America. For information about obtaining permission to reprint material from MLA book publications, send your request by mail (see address below), e-mail (permissions@mla.org), or fax (646 458-0030).

Library of Congress Cataloging-in-Publication Data

[Bekenntnisse einer giftmischerin, von ihr selbst geschrieben. English]
Confessions of a poisoner, written by herself / translated and introduced by Raleigh Whitinger and Diana Spokiene.
p. cm.—(Texts and translations ; 27)
ISBN 978-1-60329-065-4 (pbk. : alk. paper)
1. Autobiographical fiction, German—Translations into English.
2. Epistolary fiction, German—Translations into English. 3. Women—Germany—Fiction. 4. Berlin (Germany)—Social life and customs—Fiction.
I. Whitinger, Raleigh, 1944- II. Spokiene, Diana.
PT1799.A1B3713 2009
833'.6–dc22 2009040455

Texts and Translations 27
ISSN 1079-2538

Cover illustration: *Portrait of Countess Augusta von Reuss-Ebersdorf and Lobenstein, half-length, as Artemisia* (1775), painted by Johann Heinrich Tischbein the Elder

Printed on recycled paper

Published by The Modern Language Association of America
26 Broadway, New York, New York 10004-1789
www.mla.org

CONTENTS

INTRODUCTION

In 1803 an enthusiastic reading public descended on Berlin's rapidly proliferating bookstores and lending libraries in search of the novel translated here as *Confessions of a Poisoner, Written by Herself*, an anonymously published, fictional autobiography in letter form. Readers were eager to learn further details in the case of a recently apprehended real-life serial killer on whom the book was believed to be based. Yet they soon found themselves scandalized and outraged to see revealed, behind the appearance of a woman's respectable integration into the finer circles of their capital city, a shockingly frank account of a struggle for independence and fulfillment that led through a maze of promiscuous, criminal, and murderous acts. After two printings and a brief flurry of speculation about the identity and gender of the anonymous author, the book was consigned to a neglect broken only by reeditions of the German original in 1923 (by Gustav Gugitz) and 1988 (by Frank Dietschreit)—the latter heavily abridged and both now out of print.

Yet the novel merits the renewed interest it has recently begun to awaken, not only as an entertaining read but also as a document of various developments in German and European culture and literature since the late eighteenth century. Its mix of the humorous and the macabre amuses, as it exposes the dark side of the Prussian capital's newly enlightened cultural life. With ironic psychological subtlety, it depicts a young woman so well schooled by her father's world in the triumph of performed appearance over substance that she is able to fashion a seductive narrative of her own manipulated innocence and victimization. The novel is rich in glimpses of the cultural life of a city increasingly caught up in the intellectual and literary developments of modern Europe. The *Confessions* cites a host of leading authors, philosophers, and educators of the day, and it comments critically on citizens who eagerly forsake reality for the fantasy worlds of popular books and theater, on intellectual posing, and on the ostentatious accumulation of superficial cultural capital. In addition, it provides a pivotal perspective on German and European literature since the late 1700s. While echoing influential French, English, and German texts of its time, it anticipates trends in subsequent generations of epistolary novels, literary confessions, and narratives of formation (bildungsromane). It offers in particular a point of departure for considering the situation of women in the social, cultural, and literary context of the day. The mystery and uncertainty that still surround the novel's authorship link it to many works—by men and women alike, their authorship known, anonymous, or pseudonymous—that reflect or contest the images of women and women writers in modern, male-dominated culture.

The *Confessions* takes the form of a long letter, divided into three books, written by the narrator to her esteemed friend

Julie Z. As it is intended to be read only on the demise of its author, readers are left to surmise that the creator of the long epistolary confession has either succumbed to the physical toll of her adventurous life or—less likely—been brought to justice by the police and courts. The letter consists of the narrating woman's admission and explanation of her guilt in the murder, by poison, of three people: her husband, her aunt, and a business partner. But this fulfillment of the title's promise of a female poisoner begins only near the end of the second book. Two-thirds of the work is given to an extensive life story in which the protagonist recounts her fortunes since birth, analyzing the factors of upbringing, education, and social outlooks that led to her descent into the sequence of moral transgressions that set the stage for crime and homicide.

She recalls a childhood and youth seduced by her father's world and values. She soon becomes alienated from her mother, a woman whose early coercion into a conventional, arranged marriage leaves her prone to moral equivocation, ostentatious piety, and the selfish pursuit of the pleasures afforded by alcohol and illicit sex. The preteen daughter is steered by an amoral and manipulative father who carelessly encourages her interest in novels and the theater, both so popular in that generation's Berlin. Approaching womanhood and poorly guided in matters of sex, the girl too quickly seeks a romantic situation; is seduced by an older man, a French count; and suffers an unwanted pregnancy and traumatic abortion. Soon afterward, she becomes an accessory after the fact to her father's poisoning of his wife and, even as she puts on a successful show of participation in the Protestant faith and the finer social circles of her capital city, his willing bedfellow. Following her father's death, she combines years of social climbing with clandestine romantic liaisons, a split life of outward propriety and hidden depravity that continues until her marriage to a ranking civil servant. That union is soon strained by her unfulfilled longing to bear a child and by the various affairs in which she seeks amusement and satisfaction. Then, desperately in love with a handsome and altruistic young cousin of her husband, she ultimately resorts to her father's methods and poisons her ailing husband. In this, she evades detection by all but her intended lover, who, wracked by guilt over his unintentional role in the murder, takes his own life. Greed and a desperate need for diversion and pleasure motivate the protagonist's subsequent actions, and what ensues is a debilitating sequence of sensual adventures, the murder of her wealthy but ailing aunt, the involvement with a shady Jewish business partner in various forms of criminal activity, and the lethal poisoning of a partner in financial skulduggery. At her letter's end she is a prematurely worn woman, insightful to the point of cynicism; disillusioned by her society's superficial morality, which has fostered in her the avarice that she sees as an inborn human inclination; and full of advice on how the education of young women and more vigorous regulation of modern urban life might forestall such waywardness.

The novel owed its initial popularity to the eagerness of readers to learn more about the sensational case of Countess Charlotte Ursinus, a Berlin privy councillor's widow who allegedly, between 1779 and 1803, poisoned several people, including her long-ailing husband, her aunt, various friends, and a lover. By 1803 she had been imprisoned despite the lack of proof of her guilt. Her case was the subject of many works of that time and was later depicted in the second volume of the *Neue Pitaval* (1842; "The New Pitaval"), by Julius Hitzig and Wilhelm Häring, in which she was portrayed as a woman of mystery and a leading light of Berlin's high society. In 1804, she was the subject of a book entitled "The Assassin, Including a Confession of Her Sins, from the Papers of the Poisoner U———s: A True Novel, Written by Herself," by Ferdinand Arnold, who felt that the Unger house's publication of the sensational *Confessions of a Poisoner* had undermined interest in his own, explicitly fact-based book.

The anonymous novel disappointed readers' hopes to learn more about the countess; it also shocked readers with a female protagonist so at odds with the paragons of female virtue and submissive renunciation that populated beloved literary works of the day. As a result, it found few readers sympathetic to its criticism of the social and cultural life in Berlin or to its contesting what was then considered the virtuous calling of women and the refinement of their sexual nature. Yet the novel provides informative and often amusing scenes of the life of Berlin then. It provides an illuminating perspective on the emergence of a modern and urban Germany usually associated with the turn of the twentieth century. By addressing urban growth in Germany's most important cultural center around 1800, it engages in a discussion of the larger question of the city as cultural space.

Striking in German literature of that time is the portrayal of the city as the site of both progress and regression, a view most prominent in the works of Jean-Jacques

Rousseau. The poisoner's *Confessions* addresses several aspects of this view: the contrast between rural and urban life, for example, where the city represents the growing threat of civilization and a rapidly changing relation to traditional values. This critical perspective on life in the great German metropolis is bound up with the view of urban Berlin as a site of social detachment, of liberation from existing social conventions and norms, a kind of nonregulated space that can foster new outlooks and create new possibilities for action (see Erlin, "Urban Experience"; Spokiene, "Identität"). Not surprisingly, with regard to the ideal of the virtuous woman and the new bourgeois model of the family around 1800, in which women are assigned to the private domestic sphere, this liberation is often viewed in negative terms. In *Confessions of a Poisoner*, the city is a place of danger, populated by duplicitous, immoral, and thieving citizens, a place where no ideal woman should want to be. At the same time, the city is a territory suited to the exploration of alternatives to the dominant concept of bourgeois identity and open to the construction of competing gender roles.

The *Confessions* also provides an exemplary reflection of the emerging consumerism that critics note in eighteenth-century Germany and the role of consumerism in the identity formation of the German middle class (see Erlin, "Useless Subjects"; Purdy; Wurst). Although the German states of the late eighteenth century were economically and commercially underdeveloped in comparison with England and France, they were nevertheless the site of an increasingly complex consumer culture, one that affected social differentiation among members of the middle class. The novel comments on modern forms of culture and consumption such as domestic entertainment and the different forms of sociability. It portrays the popular turn to new leisure-time activities such as nature walks, spa visits, and landscape gardening. It gives a glimpse of the growing bourgeois enthusiasm for art, music, and travel as forms of entertainment, as well as literature—and, more generally, print culture—as a source of diversion and creative self-expression, of imaginative self-identification in an increasingly anonymous modern society. In this context, the novel provides a perspective on the central role played by women in the creation of everyday culture. While the patriarchal society confined women's activity to the domestic sphere, the combination of those household activities with the new forms of consumption provided women with a growing influence on public taste in matters of culture.

In rich detail the novel shows the cultural life of a city caught up in intellectual and literary change. Readers are offered glimpses of medical practices and legal procedure, and of the anti-Semitic stereotyping of assimilated Jews in the city's financial circles—the latter passages among those that the 1988 edition of the German original chose to omit. More prominent—and also shortened or missing in the 1988 edition—are the commentaries on the intellectual interests of the newly enlightened citizenry and the concomitant ill effects on the upbringing and education of its female population. There are extensive references to the reading of an increasingly literate public, to the public's mania for the theater and its embrace of new directions in philosophy, education, and child rearing, always with an acute eye for the ostentatious accumulation of cultural capital that accompanies such trends.

It mentions the weak imitations—by Johann Formey, for example—of Rousseau's 1762 *Émile; or, On Education* that sprang up in Berlin, and it comments on the theorists, like Johann Friedrich Campe and Peter Villaume, whose ideas of child upbringing were so influential in Berlin families. At great length it discusses the novels of Samuel Richardson and the deleterious effect of their vision of virtue and romance on a readership already inclined to mistake idealistic fantasy for reality. One episode tells of the enthusiasm for evening seminars offered by local scholars to explain the philosophical writings of Immanuel Kant; another mentions the competition in status-conscious social circles to curry the favor and enjoy the company of prominent men of letters.

These references to the culture of the day are part of a greater and more complex network of formal and thematic elements that link the female poisoner's narrative to works of European and German literature in the late 1700s. Various lines of comparison can be pursued. Readers might note thematic similarities of this text to narratives or bildungsromane that likewise trace an individual's descent into murder under the influence of social pressure or that attend in psychologically astute detail to inner workings of deviation: Friedrich von Schiller's *Ein Verbrecher aus verlorener Ehre* ("The Criminal from Lost Honor"), for example, or Karl Phillip Moritz's *Anton Reiser*. Yet a more complex interplay of allusions and citations links these confessions to a body of both seminal and typical contributions to the European and German novel in the eighteenth century that focus on the problems and potentials of female development.

This work belongs to a broader discourse on the emergence and questioning of fixed images and concepts of gender that prevail through the ensuing centuries and that give voice in particular to criticism of the limitations or perversions that such stereotypes impose on women. It is interesting to read the *Confessions* against contemporary writings that played a major role in establishing such images—by Rousseau, Goethe, Schiller, Gotthold Ephraim Lessing, Campe, and Johann Gottlieb Fichte. Like many works by male and female authors that offer female protagonists (Christian Gellert, Sophie von La Roche, Friederike Helene Unger, Sophie Mereau), the *Confessions* anticipates the ensuing century of authors and texts struggling with the confining images and roles of women (cf. Becker-Cantarino; Joeres, *Respectability* and "That Girl").

In this context, the names Samuel Richardson, Rousseau, and Goethe loom especially large and provide a revealing perspective on this novel's critical dialogue with major trends of its day in the literary portrayal of women. With a combination of direct citations, allusions, formal elements, and elements of plot and theme, the *Confessions of a Poisoner* evokes for readers, then and now, those authors' works and works influenced by them. It evokes them especially with regard to the portrayal of the tribulations and triumphs of female protagonists—always with a negative, subversive twist, with a parodic thurst that unmasks as illusion the earlier idealistic visions of sacrifice, compromise, and conciliation.

Richardson and his influence are called to mind not only by the epistolary form of this text but also by the direct references to his novels. Looking back at her early adolescence, the protagonist recalls her fateful turn, after her misguided enthusiasm for the theater had already left her confused about the boundary between performed illusion and reality, to Richardson's *Pamela; or, Virtue Rewarded* (1740–42), *Clarissa Harlowe* (1747–48), and *Sir Charles Grandison* (1753). To these fictional literary portrayals of a woman's virtue rewarded by noble male heroes or of her grieving renunciation in the face of misfortune at the hands of calculating men, the narrating poisoner attributes a deleterious effect on her own expectations and demands in life. From early on, her narrative shows Richardson's ideals to be illusions. They appeal to the naive adolescent yet are at odds with reality. The poisoner's story is a lurid account of the ideals of female virtue and romantic love gone wrong.

Richardson's *Clarissa* had been a major influence on Sophie La Roche's 1771 epistolary novel *Geschichte des Fräuleins von Sternheim* ("The History of Lady Sophia Sternheim"), a work that critics consider seminal in the emergence of German domestic fiction, the woman's novel (*Frauenroman*), and even the female bildungsroman. Yet La Roche's heroine, Sophie, moves beyond Clarissa's submissive sacrifice only to compromise. She grows to a conservative acceptance of her place in the domestic sphere of the male master. Her acceptance does express the era's attempt to legitimize the narrowness of women's sphere (Hausen), but it also harbors subtle signs of a growing female independence (Joeres, "That Girl"; cf. Bach 173; Beaujean 15; Bovenschen 190–200; Hohendahl; Kontje 39–40). By contrast, the 1803 poisoner's narrative promises a similar plot line, only to turn it in a less conciliatory direction. Like Richardson's Clarissa with Lovelace, like La Roche's Sophie with Lord Derby, the poisoner endures an early crisis of virtue threatened by seduction at the hands of her tutor. Yet the survival and moral triumph of Clarissa and Sophie are glaringly absent as this poisoner's story unfolds. The early sexual misadventure makes her easy prey for her father's incestuous desires, and their lurid affair is the cause of the barrenness that prevents her from fulfilling her ideal of motherhood, making her life an empty search for diversion and status that repeatedly leads to deception, promiscuity, and crime.

A Rousseau novel plays an equally influential role as German domestic fiction evolves from La Roche to this unusual 1803 text. Rousseau's *Julie; or, The New Heloise* (1761) also influenced La Roche's popular *Sternheim* novel, with its portrayal of a likewise compromising heroine who progresses through conflict and crisis from obedient daughter to conciliatory wife and mother. The 1803 poisoner text refers in challenging fashion to it as well. The confessing narrator addresses her letter to her revered friend Julie Z., who strongly resembles her Rousseauesque namesake as a paragon of traditional female virtue who has lived the ideal of wife, mother, and household manager without lament of the sacrifice and cost. The surname initial Z may be intended to place Julie at the end of that ideal's lineage. It is against that quiet ideal that a rebellious, criminal woman asserts her detailed account. Thus, if the first German emulators of Rousseau's novel—La Roche in *Sternheim*, Friederike Helene Unger in *Julchen Grünthal*—tended more to resemble than refute it, the *Confessions of a Poisoner* offers a darkly distorted echo of it. This echo is signaled first by the narrator's misadventure with Vaudreuil, the expatriate French nobleman hired as her tutor. The episode recalls the love of Rousseau's noble Julie for her bourgeois teacher but reverses the class relation between the two lovers and lacks the enduring trajectory of the pupil-teacher affair in Rousseau's novel toward compromise and conciliation.

With these evocations of Richardson and Rousseau, the poisoner's confessions emphatically state their deviation from the ideals of female development that prevail in the early stages of German women's fiction. They counter the dominant image of the obediently submissive heroine with an unrepentantly independent account of a woman's disastrous misadventures, repeatedly recalling yet refuting those earlier visions of virtue triumphant and noble, selfless sacrifice to the ideal of the family unit.

Rousseau is present elsewhere in the dense intertextual network of this poisoner's letter, not merely where reference is made to Formey's novel or when the story calls to mind an episode in Rousseau's *Confessions* in which a reading-mad father has an unhealthy effect on the imagination of his offspring. The title itself, with its use of *Bekenntnisse*, signals another complex line of allusions to and echoes of Rousseau and others. That term links the poisoner narrative on the one hand to Rousseau's own *Confessions* of 1766 to 1770 and the ensuing tradition of literary confessions that extends even to the complex feminist confessions of the twentieth century. It links it on the other hand to Goethe's *Wilhelm Meisters Lehrjahre* (*The Apprenticeship of Wilhelm Meister*) of 1795–96 and the variations on the male and female bildungsroman that sprang up in its wake around and after 1800, by recalling an inlaid text in Goethe's novel that likewise bears the title "Bekenntnisse."

Rousseau's *Confessions* was translated into German in 1782 as *Bekenntnisse*, by Friederike Helene Unger (1751–1813), the wife and coworker of Johann Friedrich Unger (1753–1804), in whose publishing house the *Confessions of a Poisoner* was to appear. The title's echo of *Bekenntnisse* combines with the poisoner's early appeal to her dear Julie to underline her story's provocative challenge to Rousseau. Simply by presenting itself as a work of "confessions" by a woman writer, the poisoner text announces its opposition to the prevailing perspective on the nature and role of women. With this step, a woman appropriates the genre of a famous male writer known for his ardent insistence on woman's adherence to her natural and proper sphere and for his disdain of writing women (Kontje 6–7), soliciting as she does so the tacit sympathy of an embodiment of Rousseau's ideals. Her *Confessions* follows the Rousseauesque tradition as well in its attention to grasping and defining the sexual side of the individual. Although the work is not singular among the many Rousseau emulators of the day as the sexual confessions of a woman rather than a man, it compares more favorably with the original than many other such imitations in the self-critical candor with which its author admits the errors and weaknesses that mark her development.

The English word *confessions* has three German equivalents, and the occurrence of *Bekenntnisse* in the title of both the poisoner's letter and the German translation of Rousseau's work marks the letter's modernity, its turn from the religiously tinged *Beichte* or the legalistic *Geständnis*—both terms translatable as "confession." *Bekenntnisse* indicates a focus not on deference to existing authorities and orders but on grasping or knowing (*kennen*) the authentic, subjective, modern self. As a confession by a woman, of course, it also instantiates tensions and contradictions that emerge in feminist narratives in the late twentieth century (Felski), above all with its mix of liberation attempted and oppression revealed. Thus it is arguably an instance of a female text anticipating feminist literature (Evans). In this early work, too, the drive to confess is a contradictory one; it aims to discover an independent real self, to achieve intimacy and revelation, yet at the same time it subverts or thwarts that impulse. Like later feminist confessions, the poisoner's narrative, with its intimation of female authorship and readership, bears witness to a nascent, female bourgeois subjectivity exploring its emotions and seeking self-understanding. Instead of merely admitting guilt, this subjectivity "symbolizes a private assertion of freedom [that] may challenge rather than conform to existing social norms" (Felski 87). It effectively criticizes specific problems experienced by women to suggest its possible "role in the process of identity formation and cultural change" (92). Yet it can also appear simply to reveal rather than overcome women's alienation, oppression, and manipulation by a society of dubious values; it can appear to be a self-pitying attempt to manipulate the facts and shift the blame. Any objective reader of these confessions might think that cunning is the only recourse that nature and society leave a woman who is deprived of power, that she can purchase freedom only by criminal means. Yet once stated by the narrator herself, that reading cannot but become an object of critical reflection.

The poisoner's narrative is of course not the only work linked to Goethe's seminal bildungsroman *The Appren-*

ticeship of Wilhelm Meister. Several works in various ways echo and counter his vision of the gifted individual's fulfilling individual development, social integration, and harmonious marriage. Ludwig Tieck, Friedrich Schlegel, and Novalis (Friedrich von Hardenberg) led the way, around 1800, with a succession of novels that acknowledge a debt to Goethe's masterpiece while striving to outdo his innovative openness of form and counter his vision of the artistic male protagonist's integration into the father's world. Nor is the poisoner's *Confessions* unique in its shift to a female protagonist's struggle with the possibility of *Bildung*. Female-oriented narratives by male and female authors alike parallel the early evolution of the male-centered bildungsroman. La Roche's *Sternheim* and Unger's *Julchen Grünthal* begin a two-century tradition of female bildungsromane that regender or challenge the *Wilhelm Meister* model (cf. Blackwell; Hirsch; Kleinbord-Labovitz; Kontje). But with its title the poisoner text calls attention to a specific sequence of works that focus on a critical dialogue about how Goethe's novel portrays the writing, confessing woman and her prospects of *Bildung*—of fulfilling individual formation and integration in a male-dominated world.

The sixth book of Goethe's novel contains an inlaid text, "Bekenntnisse einer schönen Seele" ("Confessions of a Beautiful Soul"), in which a woman recounts her life of renunciation and retreat from the conventionally expected status of a woman as acquiescent spouse, nurturing mother, and mistress of the practical and spiritual needs of the domestic sphere. Goethe agreed with the view of Rousseau, Campe, and Schiller regarding the dilettantism and substandard quality of women's writing, as is evident in his correspondence and collaboration at this time with Schiller (Bürger 19–31; Kontje 7–8). The narrating "beautiful soul" in his novel outlines a woman's fate that is much in line with the submissive, renunciative heroines of earlier novels by Richardson, Rousseau, and La Roche. The story of the "beautiful soul" is a subtext in Goethe's male bildungsroman, and the response of its female narrator to a duplicitous social reality that hinders the ideal harmony of inclination and duty, of sensuality and reason, pleads for a sympathetic acceptance of her renunciation of her conventional role as a selfless act of moral rectitude.

The *Confessions of a Poisoner* counters Goethe's "beautiful soul" with a pointedly more authentic account ("written by herself") of quite a different woman, whose struggle for integration as spouse, mother, and muse of the household and social circle exposes the perverting impact of patriarchy's demands and expectations. It offers a female bildungsroman that shows integration only partially and illusorily achieved. The narrator's outward success as a woman ever in control of the social intercourse of the city's finer circles is offset by a desire for motherhood doomed from the first by her traumatic seduction by popular notions of love and romance and twisted by that loss into a compensatory drive for fulfillment that takes her down the path of corruption and—following her father's example—murder.

The *Confessions of a Poisoner* also precedes by three years another controversial novel that even more pointedly echoes Goethe's novel and counters, with a woman speaking for herself, his rendition of a fictional female narrator's views: *Bekenntnisse einer schönen Seele; von ihr selbst geschrieben*) (1806; "Confessions of a Beautiful Soul, Written by Herself"). Like the poisoner's confessions, these are published anonymously, likewise with the publishing house of Johann Friedrich Unger, and likewise evoking but countering the notions of womanhood in Goethe's "beautiful soul" narrative. The 1806 *Confessions*—it was reprinted in 1991 but awaits English translation—represents an emphatically female perspective. Instead of pleading, like Goethe's story, for sympathetic understanding of its beautiful soul's renunciation of the full life of a proper woman, it argues that retreat from convention into friendship with another woman is a perfectly viable option for an intelligent female. These confessions too are the cause of controversy and discussion. In addition to shedding light on that era's views on female writing, they prompted speculation about the identity and gender of the authors of both the 1806 and 1803 anonymous confessions.

Critics and readers today suspect the hand of a woman or women behind both confessions, but they did not in the early 1800s. By the end of the eighteenth century, it had become common for women authors to resort to anonymous and pseudonymous publication, because of women's loss of status and exclusion from the public sphere. The prevailing ideology about women constructed a notion of their nature and function that reduced them to virtuous guardians of the domestic domain. A form of "gender censorship" in literary production was the result (Becker-Cantarino). Those writing women who remained discreetly within the proper bounds embodied the ideal; those who entered into the manly sphere of intellectual pursuits were branded dangerous dilettantes, especially if they went beyond traditionally female themes and topics. A false male name on the title page of a book, or no name, offered the adventurous woman writer a shield from derision or attack. That male authors commonly offered the letters or personal confessions of fictional but ostensibly authentic women appears to have combined with the level of provocation involved in both *Confessions* to render a curious public and critics alike disinclined to entertain the notion that a woman could have written either book.

Support for female authorship of *Confessions of a Poisoner* at that time was fleeting, soon forgotten. Male readers who approved of the novel assumed that a man had created this exposure of female depravity lurking behind the appearance of virtue, despite the feminist elements of a text in which a woman possesses a self-ironic, critical eye for ills for which conventions and values prevalent in the world of the fathers are consistently shown to be responsible.

Goethe was fascinated by the book and eager to publish a review of it (*Goethes Briefe* 328 [letter to Eichstädt, 13 Oct. 1803]). At one point, he asked his friend Carl Friedrich Zelter (1758–1832) about the author's identity, assuming that it had to be a man, whom he proclaimed to be an "able fellow" in every respect (275 [letter to Zelter, 29 Aug. 1803]). Zelter responded that *Confessions of a Poisoner* was the work of Friedrich Buchholz (1768–1843), at that time a struggling academic and author who was editing political writings for the Unger publishing house. Buchholz had already published a historical novel entitled *Bayard: Dedicated to the Officers of the Prussian Army*. He went on to write several other works and to have attributed to him several works that were published anonymously between 1800 and 1835, including both the 1803 *Confessions of a Poisoner* and the 1806 *Confessions of a Beautiful Soul*.

Regarding the 1806 confessions, Goethe noted its allusion to his own "Confessions of a Beautiful Soul" and commented critically on the near certainty of its male authorship (Zantop, Afterword 386–87). He argued that the author had used the "Confessions" to pursue the question of how a woman could save and maintain her individuality and character in the face of the complex realities of her milieu. He saw that work's female narrator as a patently invented "female man" (he uses the term "Männin" [Rev. of "Bekenntnisse" 375]), who writes in a way quite at odds with how a "woman of spirit and feeling" would actually write. Like other critics of the time, he finds the writing dominated more by "reason and rationality" than by "passion" and totally lacking in the "natural feeling," the "loving character," the "charming presentation," and "all those other good features" in which women's writing is so rich (367, 384; my trans.). The 1806 *Confessions* is dominated by the cool, distanced, rational tone of an overly refined man of the world and therefore completely lacking in femininity.

Among the literary lights of the day, only Christoph Martin Wieland (1733–1813) expressed the notion that a woman might have written *Confessions of a Poisoner*. Yet his proposal is as disparaging to women as is the claim that only a man could have written with such astute and rational insight. Wieland soon abandoned the idea, bowing to the prevailing wisdom that accepted Buchholz's authorship. Inspired both by the novel's sensational popularity and by the mystery of its authorship, he composed a short story entitled "Rechtfertigung der berühmten Frau von Maintenon gegen die höchst ungerechte Anklage: Gezogen aus einem durch die berüchtigten Bekenntnisse einer Giftmischerin veranlaßten zufälligen Gespräche" ("A Justification of the Famous Madame de Maintenon against the Most Unjust Accusation: From a Chance Conversation Brought About by the Infamous Confessions of a Poisoner") in which he refutes Goethe's assumption that only male abilities could have negotiated the complexities of the *Confessions*. Yet he does so in a manner that places women writers in a similarly ungenerous light. The story's Herr Y expounds on the novel to the gentlemen of his company after the ladies of the gathering have obediently retreated to an adjoining room to prevent the more adventurous among them from further involvement with such an unseemly book. Herr Y holds the view that only a woman could have written in such a self-serving way. He sees her evading her conscience and covering the moral ugliness of her deeds with forced rationalizations. He also notes her inept grasp of historical facts, as when her anecdote about the duke of Lauzun mistakenly substitutes Henrietta of England for the duchess of Montpensier, a blunder that proves female authorship. After learning of Zelter's claim that Buchholz was the author of the *Confessions of a Poisoner*, however, Wieland abandoned publication of his story, and it did not appear until 1913.

Buchholz's authorship remained unchallenged for longer still, even though the source of Zelter's assertion was never known and both anonymous *Confessions* are obviously unlike Buchholz's acknowledged publications in theme and style. While researchers are now inclined to attribute the 1806 *Confessions* to a prominent woman author, similar speculation regarding *Confessions of a Poisoner* awaits conclusive archival and textual verification. As early as the 1820s, accounts by Carl W. O. A. Schindel and by Georg Hamberger and Johann Meusel suggested that the 1806 *Confessions of a Beautiful Soul* might have been the product of a collaboration between Buchholz and Friederike Helene Unger, a Rousseau expert, the publisher's wife, and the acknowledged author of several women's narratives. Schindel, considered the most trusted source at that time, includes it among Unger's works and suggests that Buchholz might merely have helped with editorial revisions and allowed his name to stand in order to shield the illustrious and polemically active Frau Unger from attacks by moralists and literary adversaries (376–81). A century later, those possibilities were raised in Max Schneider's anthology of German titles, which lists Buchholz, Unger, and Charlotte von Ahlefeld (1781–1849) as authors of three allegedly different *Confessions of a Beautiful Soul* (64). Not until 1986 did Magdalene Heuser's analysis of the work pursue a comparison of thematic and stylistic elements to posit Friederike Helene Unger as the author. Her speculation still lacks concrete corroborating evidence. While no evidence indicates that Unger ever referred to the *Confessions* in her letters, Buchholz later *did*—according to Karl Goedeke's survey—acknowledge his authorship of both *Confessions*. Since the late 1980s, Susanne Zantop has espoused the cause of Unger's authorship of the *Beautiful Soul* text. Her 1991 reprint of that 1806 novel places Unger on the title page, albeit in square brackets. Her afterword points to aspects of Unger's background, literary polemics, and involvement with the financial survival of the Unger publishing house after her husband's death in 1804 that speak to the likelihood of her authorship. Yet Zantop's arguments leave the issue in the limbo of plausible speculation, as do the assumptions and claims of subsequent commentaries (e.g., Becker-Cantarino 95n5; Lehmstedt 117).

Recent criticism has also engaged in the Buchholz-Unger debate with regard to the *Confessions of a Poisoner*. Into the 1960s and 1970s, Buchholz research accepted Zelter's claim without question (e.g., Bahrs; Schäfer). In 1988, however, the editor of the most recent—but abridged—German edition of *Confessions of a Poisoner* found it so accurate and sensitive in giving voice to a self-conscious woman that he was tempted to doubt its male authorship. He went on to note the striking resemblance between the two *Confessions*, above all in their literary tone and their presentation of a free and self-determined female personality (Dietschreit 152–53). His suggestions parallel those of Heuser, Zantop, and Mark Lehmstedt regarding the *Beautiful Soul* text, and these positions find further support in a recent analysis of *Confessions of a Poisoner* that, in addition to the thematic similarities that Heuser found linking the 1806 *Confessions* to other works by Unger, uses computer analysis to show similarities in sentence length, paragraph length, word choice, and intertextual allusion (Spokiene, "Was bleibt"). All these speculations still await archival corroboration. At present, both *Confessions* are tentatively included among the official titles of Friederike Helene Unger, even though the possibility of male authorship has not been ruled out and Unger's authorship has yet to be proved.

There is a virtue to this impasse. It makes the *Confessions of a Poisoner* a point of departure for closer consideration of the entire range of late-eighteenth-century works—of male or female, of known, unknown, or still-disputed authorship—that reflect the development and doubts of that era's conceptions of women and women writers and thus deal with issues such as self-censorship, "gender censorship," anonymity, and pseudonymity, where writings by or about women are concerned. With Buchholz's authorship asserted yet in doubt, with Unger's authorship still a matter of speculation, readers are left to ponder the work's relation to both traditions. The anonymity, sensation, and outrage that prevailed through the work's first year and first two printings are a striking illustration, for example, of the limitations imposed both on women writers and on any author venturing a position on women's nature and status that featured female figures at odds with prevailing ideals. As a work of still-undetermined authorship, it invites consideration of a broader German and European context of anonymous and pseudonymous writings, many of which are instances of the widespread phenomenon of necessarily hidden (female) authorship, of the need of works that challenged prevailing views on women to resort to self-censoring concealment behind an unknown or an allegedly male identity to bring the woman's voice to the public (cf. Becker-Cantarino).

The short-lived initial debate about the gender of the novel's anonymous author reveals the notions prevalent then about women writers. The two prominent spokesmen of the opposing sides, Wieland and Goethe, both argue in terms that discount women when it comes to such categories as rational argument, self-critical assessment of moral shortcomings, adroit manipulation of complex plot, and mastery of historical details. No less eloquent is the fact that the mere and unfounded assertion of male provenance ends the debate for over a century.

Most important, the attempts in recent years to trace the 1803 *Confessions* back to the pen of Friederike Helene Unger represent merely a first step in an enlightening process of contrasting this text with a wide range of works of its generation that share its focus on a female protagonist or its substantial critical attention to the problematic issues of women's nature and status. Such a survey would establish a more detailed picture of how the anonymous *Confessions* relates in its construction of gender roles and identity to other well-known works in which (other?) male authors offer female protagonists, narrators, or writers. The work at first glance appears misogynist: behind the proper lady and muse of the cultural circle lurks a conniving and lustful creature ready to deceive and murder for gain and independence. She narrates her life in a self-serving manner. At second glance, of course, readers will note that the male creator of this text is not without profeminist inclinations. He accords the narrating woman a high degree of perceptivity and acuity, as well as self-irony, and he makes clear from the outset that the father's world is implicated in her behavior.

The survey would also foster a more extensive study of other female-authored narratives on the *Bildung* of women. More than advancing the rediscovery of Unger (cf. Giesler; Heuser; Krimmer; Lehmstedt; Spokiene, "Was bleibt"; Zantop, "Friederike Helene Unger" and Afterword), it would involve a broader context of women's writing—for example, by La Roche, Therese Huber, Bettine von Arnim, Sophie Mereau, Dorothea Schlegel, and Johanna von Schopenhauer—and an attempt to trace in these works features and characteristics that are further developed by women writers throughout the nineteenth century. This survey could involve French and English as well as German texts, with examples of female bildungsromane through to Simone de Beauvoir, Doris Lessing, and Christa Wolf, or with instances of anonymously or pseudonymously publishing women such as Mary Shelley, the Brontës, and George Eliot. It would also promote an awareness of common or recurring features of women's writing (cf. Lersch; Stephan) and invite reflection on whether the similarities to female-authored books speak for or against the possibilities of a woman's hand behind the *Confessions of a Poisoner*.

Thus the uncertainty of its authorship enhances this unusual and forgotten novel's significance and interest. The work is amusing, even in its more gruesome episodes, with its wittily unmasking description of a newly emerging modern Berlin, as well as with its creation of a narrator who simultaneously reveals and exploits the talents of posing and dissembling in which her father's world has schooled her. The *Confessions* has for many readers a further appeal, which grows in accordance with their acquaintance with the well-known writers whom it cites, evokes, and augments. For those studying the emergence of the modern novel in late-eighteenth-century Europe, it holds a wealth of perspectives: on the development of genres such as confessions, epistolary novel, and bildungsroman; on the emergence and evolution of themes such as the prospects of female *Bildung* and the fortunes of the woman writer; and on problematic research projects such as the recuperation of neglected women writers and the discourse on defining the inherent signature of individual authors, both male and female.

Works Cited

Arnold, Ferdinand. *Die Meuchelmörderin, nebst der Beichte ihrer Sünden aus den Papieren der Giftmischerin U...s: Ein wahrer Roman, von ihr selbst geschrieben*. Quedlinburg: Basse, 1804. Print.

Bach, Adolf. "Sophie von La Roche und ihre Stellung im deutschen Geistesleben des 18. Jahrhunderts." *Zeitschrift für Deutschkunde* 40 (1926): 165–82. Print.

Bahrs, Kurt. *Friedrich Buchholz, ein preußischer Publizist, 1768–1843*. 1907. Vaduz: Kraus, 1965. Print.

Beaujean, Marion. "Das Bild des Frauenzimmers im Roan des 18. Jahrhunderts." *Wolffenbüttler Studien zur Aufklärung* 3 (1976): 9–28. Print.

Becker-Cantarino, Barbara. "'Gender Censorship': On Literary Production in German Romanticism." Trans. Jeanette Clausen. *Women in German Yearbook* 11 (1995): 81–97. Print.

Bekenntnisse einer Giftmischerin, von ihr selbst geschrieben. Berlin: Unger, 1803. Ed. Gustav Gugitz. Vienna: Strache, 1923. Rev. ed. Ed. Frank Dietschreit. Berlin: Ullstein, 1988. Print. *Bibliothek der deutschen Literatur: Microfiche-Gesamtausgabe nach den Angaben des Taschengoedeke*. Ed. Axel Frey. Munich: Saur, 1990. B. 45 F. Microform.

Blackwell, Jeanine. "Bildungsroman mit Dame: The Heroine in the German 'Bildungsroman' from 1770 to 1900." Diss. Indiana U, 1982. Print.

Bovenschen, Silvia. *Die imaginierte Weiblichkeit: Exemplarische Untersuchungen zu kulturgeschichtlichen und literarischen Präsentationsformen des Weiblichen*. Frankfurt am Main: Suhrkamp, 1979. Print.

Buchholz, Paul Ferdinand Friedrich. *Bayard: Den Officiren der Preußischen Armee geweiht*. Berlin: Himburg, 1801. Print.

Bürger, Christa. *Leben Schreiben: Die Klassik, die Romantik und der Ort der Frauen*. Stuttgart: Metzler, 1990. Print.

Confessions of a Poisoner. See *Bekenntnisse*

Dietschreit, Frank. Afterword. *Bekenntnisse* [1988] 148–57.

Erlin, Matt. "Urban Experience, Aesthetic Experience, and Enlightenment in G. E. Lessing's *Minna von Barnhelm*." *Monatshefte* 93.1 (2001): 20–35. Print.

———. "Useless Subjects: Reading and Consumer Culture in Eighteenth-Century Germany." *German Quarterly* 80.2 (2007): 145–65. Print.

Evans, Richard J. "The Concept of Feminism: Notes for Practicing Historians." Joeres and Maynes 247–58.

Felski, Rita. "On Confession." *Women, Autobiography, Theory: A Reader*. Ed. Sidonie Smith and Julia Watson. Madison: U of Wisconsin P, 1998. 83–95. Print.

Giesler, Birte. *Literatursprünge: Das erzählerische Werk von Friederike Helene Unger*. Göttingen: Wallstein, 2003. Print.

Goedeke, Karl August. *Grundriß der Deutschen Dichtung: Aus den Quellen*. Dresden: Ehlermann, 1900. Print.

Goethe, Johann Wolfgang von. Rev. of "Bekenntnisse einer schönen Seele, von ihr selbst geschrieben; *Melanie, das Findelkind*; *Wilhem von Dumont* von Eleutherie Holberg." *Theater und Schauspielkunst: Beiträge und Älteres*. Goethe, *Goethe Werke* 40: 367–84.

———. *Goethes Briefe: 1802, 1803*. Goethe, *Goethes Werke* 16.

———. *Goethes Werke*. 144 vols. Weimar: Böhlau, 1887–1919.Print.

Hamberger, Georg Christoph, and Johann Georg Meusel. *Das gelehrte Teutschland; oder, Lexikon der jetzt lebenden teutschen Schriftsteller*. Vol. 21. 1827. Hildesheim: Olms, 1966. Print.

Hausen, Karin. "Die Polarisierung der 'Geschlechtscharaktere'—Eine Spiegelung der Dissoziation von Erwerbs- und Familienleben." *Sozialgeschichte der Familie in der Neuzeit Europas: Neue Forschungen*. Ed. Werner Conze. Stuttgart: Klett, 1976. 363–93. Print. Trans. as "Family and Role-Division: The Polarisation of Sexual Stereotypes in the Nineteenth Century—an Aspect of the Dissociation of Work and Family." *The German Family: Essays on the Social History of the Family in Nineteenth- and*

Twentieth-Century Germany. Ed. Richard J. Evans and W. R. Lee. London: Croom Helm, 1981. 51–83.

Heuser, Magdalene. "'Spuren trauriger Selbstvergessenheit': Möglichkeiten eines weiblichen Bildungsromans um 1800: Friederike Helene Unger." *Frauensprache—Frauenliteratur? Für und Wider einer Psychoanalyse literarischer Werke*. Ed. Inge Stephan and Carl Pietzcker. Tübingen: Niemeyer, 1986. 30–42. Print.

Hirsch, Marianne. "The Beautiful Soul as Paradigm." *The Voyage In: Fictions of Female Development*. Ed. Elizabeth Abel, Hirsch, and Elizabeth Langland. Hanover: UP of New England, 1983. 23–48. Print.

Hitzig, Julius, and Wilhelm Häring. *Der Neue Pitaval: Eine Sammlung der interessantesten Criminalgeschichten aller Länder aus älterer und neuerer Zeit*. Vol. 2. Leipzig: Brockhaus, 1842. Print.

Hohendahl, Peter Uwe. "Empfindsamkeit und gesellschaftliches Bewusstsein: Zur Soziologie des empfindsamen Romans am Beispiel von *La Vie der Marianne, Clarissa, Fräulein von Sternheim* und *Werther*." *Jahrbuch der deutschen Schillergesellschaft* 6 (1972): 176–207. Print.

Joeres, Ruth-Ellen Boetcher. *Respectability and Deviance: Nineteenth-Century German Women Writers and the Ambiguity of Representation*. Chicago: U of Chicago P, 1998. Print.

———. "'That Girl Is an Entirely Different Character!' Yes, But Is She a Feminist? Observations on Sophie von La Roche's *Geschichte des Fräuleins von Sternheim*." Joeres and Maynes 137–56.

Joeres, Ruth-Ellen B., and May Jo Maynes, eds. *German Women in the Eighteenth and Nineteenth Centuries: A Social and Literary History*. Bloomington: U of Indiana P, 1986. Print.

Kleinbord-Labovitz, Esther. *The Myth of the Heroine: The Female Bildungsroman in the Twentieth Century: Dorothy Richardson, Simone de Beauvoir, Doris Lessing, Christa Wolf*. New York: Lang, 1986. Print.

Kontje, Todd. *Women, the Novel, and the German Nation, 1771–1871: Domestic Fiction in the Fatherland*. Cambridge: Cambridge UP, 1998. Print.

Krimmer, Elisabeth. "A Spaniard in the Attic: The Texture of Gender in Friederike Helene Unger's *Rosalie und Nettchen.*" *Journal of Popular Culture* 34 (2000): 209–27. Print.

La Roche, Sophie. *Geschichte des Fräuleins von Sternheim, von einer Freundin derselben aus Original-Papieren und anderen zuverlässigen Quellen gezogen.* 1771. Munich: Winkler, 1983. Print.

Lehmstedt, Mark "'Ich bin nun vollends zur Kaufmannsfrau verdorben': Zur Rolle der Frau in der Geschichte des Buchwesens am Beispiel von Friederike Helene Unger (1751–1813)." *Leipziger Jahrbuch zur Buchgeschichte* 6 (1996): 81–154. Print.

Lersch, Barbara. "Schreibende Frauen—eine neue Sprache in der Literatur?" *Diskussion Deutsch* 15 (1984): 293–313. Print.

Purdy, Daniel. *The Tyranny of Elegance: Consumer Cosmopolitanism in the Era of Goethe.* Baltimore: Johns Hopkins UP, 1998. Print.

Rousseau, Jean-Jacques. *Émile; or, On Education.* 1762. Trans. Allan Bloom. New York: Basic, 1979. Print.

———. *Julie: or, The New Heloise.* Trans. Philip Stewart and Jean Vaché. Hanover: UP of New England, 1997. Print.

Schäfer, Rütger. *Friedrich Buchholz—ein vergessener Nachläufer der Soziologie: Eine historische und bibliographische Untersuchung über den ersten Vertreter des Positivismus und des Saint-Simonismus in Deutschland.* 2 vols. Göppingen: Kümmerle, 1972. Print.

Schindel, Carl Wolfgang Otto August. *Die deutschen Schriftstellerinnen des 18. und 19. Jahrhunderts.* Vol. 2. Leipzig: Brockhaus, 1825. Print.

Schneider, Max. *Deutsches Titelbuch.* Berlin, 1927. Print.

Spokiene, Diana. "Identität durch Stadtgeschichte: Friederike Helene Ungers Briefe über Berlin (1798)." *Geschichte(n)—Erzählen: Konstruktionen von Vergangenheit in literarischen Werken deutschsprachiger Autorinnen seit dem 18. Jahrhundert.* Ed. Marianne Henn, Irmela von der Lühe, and Anita Runge. Göttingen: Wallstein, 2005. 249–64. Print.

———. "'Was bleibt...deinem Geschlecht anders übrig als die List': *Bekenntnisse einer Giftmischerin, von ihr selbst geschrieben:* Friederike Helene Unger und die Autorschaftsfrage." Diss. U of Alberta, 2004. Print.

Stephan, Inge. "Weibliche und männliche Autorschaft: Zum 'Florentin' von Dorothea Schlegel und zur 'Lucinde' von Friedrich Schlegel." *"Wen kümmert's, wer spricht?" Zur Literatur und Kulturgeschichte von Frauen von Ost und West*. Ed. Stephan, Sigrid Weigel, and Kerstin Wilhelms. Cologne: Böhlau, 1991. 83–99. Print.

[Unger, Friederike Helene]. *Bekenntnisse einer schönen Seele, von ihr selbst geschrieben*. Berlin: Unger, 1806. Ed. Susanne Zantop. Hildesheim: Olms, 1991. Print.

Unger, Friederike Helene. *Julchen Grünthal*. 1784. 3rd rev. ed. Berlin: Unger, 1798. Print.

Wieland, Christoph Martin. "Rechtfertigung der berühmten Frau von Maintenon. . . ." Ed. Bernhard Seuffert. *Zeitschrift für Bücherfreunde* 4.2 (1913): 308–14. Print.

Wurst, Karin. *Fabricating Pleasure: Entertainment and Cultural Consumption in Germany, 1770–1830*. Detroit: Wayne State UP, 2005. Print.

Zantop, Susanne. Afterword. Unger, *Bekenntnisse* 385–416.

———. "Friederike Helene Unger." *German Writers in the Age of Goethe: Sturm und Drang to Classicism*. Ed. James Hardin and Christoph E. Schweitzer. Detroit: Gale Research, 1989. 288–93. Print. Vol. 94 of *Dictionary of Literary Biography*.

NOTE ON THE TRANSLATION

The principles prevailing in this translation adhere to basic trends that translation studies sees beginning with the "German tradition" as it evolves since the end of the eighteenth century (Lefevere; Schleiermacher) and extending to the cultural turn of the late twentieth century (Berman; Robinson; Steiner). In essence, this approach holds to the notion that the translation of a literary work of an era both culturally and historically distant should not make alterations or modernizations that bring the translation into line with prevailing understandings, generic conventions, aesthetic norms, concepts of style, and commonly used images and phrases of the target language and culture. Instead, it should preserve the foreignness of the original, together with details of language and imagery that might constitute networks of theme and imagery essential to the original's text. Accordingly, this approach conceives of translation—of enacting what German terms *Übersetzung*, literally a "setting over," a transporting across a divide—not as a process meant to transcend or bridge differences between the cultures and usages of the source text and the target language and culture but as an exercise that persistently confronts its readers with the "trials" or challenges of the "foreign" (Berman), that attempts to preserve the original's linguistic signals of hidden networks of meaning and imagery, that takes its readers to another time and culture whose kinship to the present in terms of the human condition is all the more striking for the difference of the trappings in which it is embedded.

Adherence to this principle of literary translation has resulted in a work that we hope is biased more to source text than to target culture. Other than the occasional—and for readers optional—footnote, no gesture has been made to eliminate or simplify passages that might at first strike readers as dated, obscure, extraneous, or unimportant. In most instances, the translation has chosen to retain and attempt to convey references, allusions, imagery, stylistic idiosyncrasies, and verbose passages that may at first seem to detract from the story but that nevertheless play a role in how the original reveals its historical and cultural context or the character of the author, the fictive narrator, and other figures in the text.

Our first resolution was to omit nothing of the original, which might seem a platitude to those acquainted with recent decades of translation studies. Yet emphasizing it at the outset is in order, given the previous treatments of the *Confessions*. In 1988, a modernized—but only briefly accessible—edition of the original German elected to abridge the text, in particular by removing sequences that the editor found to be unimportant and digressive (Dietschreit 157). This decision resulted in the omission of virtually every passage in which the narrator commented at length on the literary and cultural interests of her day. The 1988 edition omitted passages that involved her reflections on problems of educating the female population or comments on important contemporary writers and thinkers. The net effect was to diminish the impression of her intellect and critical ability and to narrow the commentary on literary and cultural developments. Over 25 of the original's 287 pages, nine percent, were lost. The present volume has restored and translated those passages in the conviction that, while they might seem to retard the pace of the story of an emerging criminal, they remain part of the text, conveying the narrator's milieu and showing us a person who is not only aware of fashions in reading and study and cultural consumption but an able and insightful participant in them.

A similar principle of faithful inclusion has also prevailed on a smaller scale; no unusual images or cultural references were lost by a translation attempting to clarify or rationalize obscurities. For example, while some modern translators might elect to replace obscure classical references or instances of dated imagery with terms more accessible to a modern and foreign audience, this translation has retained them. We clarify only with the occasional footnote or by the use of a "translation couplet," which retains and explains the foreign or obscure phrase—on the principle that classical references inform today's readers of what Germans of the late 1700s perceived to be their cultural heritage and the marks of erudition. For terms such as "tramontane," "Egide," and "Juno Pronuba," the original is retained and clarified in the text or in a note. We also opted to avoid an excess of footnotes, leaving readers to pursue on their own some terms of significance in the late 1700s—for example, "the art of deciphering," "intension," "widows' fund," and "amphiboly." Readers are invited, further, to trace and ponder references that might come from the fictional narrator's (or author's?) tendency to unfounded cultural references—as with the reference to the "donkey in the fable" who wanted to be a chamberlain or the "Sarmatian" damsel who leapt from incarceration into her lover's waiting arms.

We resisted the temptation to impose present-day conceptions of English style on the original. Like the 1988 edition of the original, we use modern conventions of punctuation and spelling, instead of trying to concoct the illusion of quaintness with archaic orthography. Yet while attempting to leave the text as understandable to English readers as the original was to its German audience, the translation has retained the original's sentence length and hypotaxis as well as its penchant for long paragraphs. Readers will therefore be confronted with a degree of semicolon splicing that interferes with the reception of an informative text; they will find unbroken pages of narrative and reflection that may try their patience. Yet this closeness to the original was motivated by the idea that the narrator's unhalting, breathless rush of words was intentional. One concession we made to the modern reader was to insert paragraph breaks in instances of recorded and quoted dialogue between characters.

Another linguistic aspect of the original that posed a challenge to translation was its use of verbs and nouns of French and English origin—its recurring verbs with *-ieren* endings and its use of French and English cognate nouns rather than their German equivalents. By sparing its readers this dense mixing in of foreign terms, the 1988 German reedition deprived the late Enlightenment language of the original of culturally significant features, a literary language that emerged in the shadow of French and English models and was thus given to extensive borrowing, especially by those bent on exhibiting their erudition. This translation has retained many of the French phrases. Yet it had trouble finding a strategy for rendering the many borrowed verbs in a way that signaled the educated German preference then for French and English terms. The loss is compensated for by the retained French usages and by the narrator's explicit references to the mania in her circles for reading and translating other literatures.

Finally, in this translation we resisted the temptation to correct errors other than those that were clearly the result of faulty typesetting and proofreading. We also resisted the temptation to elide or alter instances of unappealing content. The narrator recalls her dealings with Moses S——, the wily Jewish businessman whom she ultimately outfoxes in their shifty financial dealings. The 1988 German edition radically shortened this episode and frequently substituted "person" for "Jew," thus reducing the recurring anti-Semitic stereotype. This episode has been translated here uncut, so readers may obtain a full picture of the narrator, the author, and their social and intellectual circles. Other passages contained blunders that call for correction or a narrative move that calls for remedy. The historical reference that wrongly substitutes Henrietta of England for the duchess of Montpensier has been retained and footnoted, because of the role it played in how contemporaries speculated on the author's gender. For the unusual paraphrase of a Shakespearean quotation, we did not insert the correct original but held to a clumsy English that was closer to the original German, in the belief that its similarity to the pre-Schlegel translations of Shakespeare contributes to the characterization of the narrator's cultural pursuits and also sheds light on the animosity between the Unger and Schlegel circles of those years.

We left the original ending intact, retaining its verbose and anticlimactic drift into commentary on the need for more rigorous policing, forensic autopsies, and coroners' inquests to forestall crime—a mark of the text's concern with ill effects of rapid urban development. The ending also shows the complexity of one of the narrator's prominent comments on the roots of her problem—namely, that she sees herself as a warning example of an education that was more masculine than feminine instead of as the victim of simply a wrong education (cf. *Bekenntnisse* [1988] 145).

The translation offered here might burden readers with a text that retards its account of criminal descent with reflections on literature and culture long past, with a narrator who slips into historical inaccuracy, dilettantish literary showmanship, and even her milieu's tendency to anti-Semitic stereotyping. Our purpose, however, was to provide a full and complex picture.The original may ramble and rationalize, but its mix of personal storytelling and literary allusion links it to prevailing traditions of fiction. The *Confessions* is an example of a modern tendency to combine the telling of the story with the story of the telling, to play its narrative off against the tradition, and to both take up and bend influences. By not adulterating the original's combination of fictive author's personal confession with her reflections on her complex world and problems, the translation preserves her attempt to assert and form her identity even as it reveals the tendency inherent in any confession to rationalize and shift moral responsibility. The translation presents the *Confessions* in full. The work may be taken merely as an amusing oddity in its daring parodic play with traditions and ideals of the German novel of the time or as an embodiment of the essentially double-leveled play of the modern bildungsroman, in both its male and female strain, with the ironic give-and-take of idealized narrative with subversive text.

Works Cited

Bekenntnisse einer Giftmischerin, von ihr selbst geschrieben. Ed. Frank Dietschreit. Berlin: Ullstein, 1988. Print.

Berman, Antoine. "Translation and the Trials of the Foreign." 1984. Venuti, *Translation Studies Reader* 276–89.

Dietschreit, Frank. Afterword. *Bekenntnisse* 148–57.

Lefevere, Andre, ed. *Translating Literature: The German Tradition from Luther to Rosenzweig*. Amsterdam: Assen, 1977. Print.

Robinson, Douglas. *Becoming a Translator: An Introduction to the Theory and Practice of Translation*. New York: Routledge, 2003. Print.

Schleiermacher, Friederich. "On the Different Methods of Translating." 1813. Trans. Sylvia Bernofsky. Venuti, *Translation Studies Reader* 43–63.

Steiner, George. "The Hermeneutic Motion." 1976. Venuti, *Translation Studies Reader* 193–98.

Venuti, Lawrence, ed. *Translations Studies Reader*. 2nd ed. New York: Routledge, 2004. Print.

Confessions of a Poisoner, Written by Herself

To the Reader of These Pages

Proving the authenticity of a piece of writing is such a difficult matter that all who have attempted it have always fallen short of their expectations, finding that the harder they try to instill belief, the more disbelief grows.

In order to avoid being accused either of my own gullibility or, worse still, of intentionally attempting to deceive, I find, as publisher of the confessions offered here, no alternative but to implore the reader as follows:

"Take all that is or appears to be factual in these confessions in such a way as to arrive in doing so at the solution of a remarkable psychological problem."

By fulfilling this humble request, gentle reader, you spare the publisher the task of explaining this work's genesis, its fortunes, and many other matters that a publisher who does not wish to appropriate an undue importance would prefer not to mention and that might well remain unsaid without in the least diminishing the worth of the piece of writing in question.

The Publisher

To Julie Z.

What am I to call you?—my friend?— To my own shadow at least I must confess that I have no friend—nor can I have one—even though I comport myself in the outer world as if I placed some value upon my friendship.— My most revered friend!— When I first saw you I was alarmed and startled by your innocence. Yes, alarm is the right word to describe the feeling that seized me when I first met you. People like you are a rarity in any case; yet for years I had given up any hope of coming to know a woman who, eschewing all false adornment, shows herself always as she is—truthful in all her ways—ardent in the pursuit of the conscientious fulfillment of her duties—unassuming in the true sense of the word—at peace with all the world—and living more for others than for herself. It was without doubt the contrast in which I stood to you that alarmed me. For basically I was alarmed about myself—about my inner ugliness—about the twisted caricature that my inner physiognomy had become. And since one cannot hate oneself, I attempted at the start to convince myself that what I took in you at first to be innocence was nothing but a product of a certain simplemindedness. But this illusion I had all too soon to abandon; for each time I saw you again I had the opportunity to notice that the feeling for what is grand and beautiful was present in you in greater purity and strength than in all my other acquaintances and that your judgment extended to matters that as a rule lie outside the realm of our thoughts. And then, revered friend, when I saw you in the circle of your family, then the scales fell from my eyes for good and all; for it was then I realized there was a compelling necessity in your innocence, your angelic goodness. I shall say nothing of your husband, but I have seen your sons. Surely you still recall how I sat there in thought, nothing able to distract or cheer me. The thought that occupied me totally was: "Had you ever had one such son, then your life would be better now." I shall return to this point more than once in my confessions. But suffice to say: knowing you forced me to reflect on myself more earnestly than I had ever done. Uncaring about all matters that had occupied me before, I think now only about how I have become what I am, and as I turn to write down my experiences, it is solely for the reason that I want to understand myself with total clarity. However I may die, these pages will come into your hands after my death; I have arranged all my affairs to ensure this will happen. You will experience horror upon horror as you read about me; but from such feelings I could not spare you if I wanted to be truthful and honest once again in my life. As to Him who judges all the world, so to you I want to reveal my inmost self. Curse me if you can. Exoneration I seek not; I would even hate any person who undertook to defend me. That I am a criminal, this I know; that I must heap crime upon crime, I know equally well. For me there will be no remorse, and far less able am I to retreat from the path I have taken. All I can bring myself to do is to avoid those whom my entire being forces me to love. With the rest of the world I shall carry on the struggle I have begun, ready to go down in defeat once my cunning is at an end. This I have vowed to do. With each step I find an abyss at my feet, and I shrink back from one and then the next, tracing a serpentine path. Heaven knows how long this will go on and how I shall ultimately fall, for fall I truly must.

First Book

Though taken by itself a person's birth may be a matter of great indifference, still it means everything when considered in its relationship to the upbringing that then at once ensues. I have reflected on this point at great length, and the result of my reflections is that I had to be born and raised by precisely the parents I had in order to turn out as I did.

My father was the notorious W——, who became a traitor to his fatherland and king. Have you ever seen a picture of Cesare Borgia? I do not know how nature goes about reviving certain forms that were long since destroyed; but I do know that no similarity can be greater than the one that existed between my father and that confirmed egotist.[1] Nor was this similarity merely a physical one. For my father, too, as far as I knew him, held nothing sacred; and had he lived in revolutionary times, or had some man with great power in this world considered

[1] Cesare Borgia (1476–1507), embodiment of Renaissance individualism in its more sinister form, was much admired by Machiavelli for his ruthless wielding of power to consolidate Italian states for the church and carve out his own principality.

it worth the trouble to smooth the way for him, then he would have gone forth as bravely and boldly as that bygone Borgia to find his place upon some throne. Never has a citizen been less at a loss for the means of making his fortune. These means lay ready in his soul even before the opportunity had presented itself for him to apply them. Whatever happened to him, he was always as self-assured as could be; he always looked as if he had long expected the most recent event to happen; he always knew what to do. The utmost in inner turmoil and the utmost in outward poise seemed to have an equal share in this character. I am sure he loved no mortal more than himself; but he always looked as if the world were too small for his goodwill. His politeness was engaging in a way I cannot define. He spoke a great deal, but always cautiously and, it always seemed to me, in a manner far more bent upon making others open and guileless than upon revealing anything of himself. As widely known as his crime was, I still never saw any sign that people hated him; the maxim holding that we might love the act of treason and despise the traitor could have been reversed in his case. Achieving this was no doubt not an easy feat for him, and his generosity helped in no small way to reconcile people's feelings in his favor, however much that generosity as well was all too much a matter of appearances. No one understood the value of money better than he did, even though he managed to make it appear as if he did not value it at all. He did not die a poor man, as much money as he did give out during the last twenty years of his life. His association with those of the finest circles was surely much to his advantage in pecuniary respects. With these people he remained on such friendly and discreet terms as to gain their trust in his tactfulness all the more. People often told me he was apprised of that social circle's most intricate affairs, and I believe it; for he was ever observant, and while on the one hand he saw human doings and dealings as a despicable game he might on occasion be moved to spurn, he still never stopped keeping a careful watch and even turning that game to his lucrative advantage. Picture my father, then, as a tall, rather lean man, pale of complexion, with large, dark eyes and a hand of exquisite beauty I even now cannot recall without interest, as I have never seen one more beautiful. He would not have gained your approval, I know; but you, like thousands upon thousands of others, would have said of him: "An interesting man!"

In my mother resided, as in most women, a contradiction that was never resolved. The underlying foundation of her character, as far as I was able to understand it, was her piety. The daughter of a clergyman from Saxony, she was married to my father at a time when she had barely begun to think of wanting a husband—so young, that is, that she was utterly incapable of contemplating the relationship she was being rushed into. My father would have been able to form and guide her for good or for ill if, for one thing, he had found anything interesting about her and if, for another, he had not been fated to be forced by exceptional circumstances from the circle of domestic happiness. He often told me himself that he found my mother's praying unbearable from the start. If I take his word for that, then I must assume that my parents never understood each other and that their relationship to each other was the same in their first year together as it was in the last. But be that as it may, I am at least certain there can be no marriage that was either more miserable or, at the same time, more convenient than theirs was. My father, in any case, had not the least pretensions or demands where my mother was concerned, and while she, in turn, was more often than not conscious of having a husband, she had not the slightest notion of what marriage really is. Since she was not without feelings of her own, she did not fail to seek recompense for enduring my father's neglect. About thirty years ago, clerics were no better than they are now; but people had a higher opinion of them back then. My mother's lover was a minister who had found it to his advantage to remain unmarried and who differed still further from his fellow clergymen by willingly playing the agreeable guest at the tables of the wealthy—something unheard of at that time, however commonplace it may be today—where he would offer up anecdotes gathered from far and wide in payment for the more tangible delicacies he was served. M——, for that was his name, more than merely turning up at my father's table, took advantage of that man's distracted way of life to make more bearable for my mother the deadly boredom consuming her. People who are pious are always more in love than those who are not, and for that reason, no doubt, M—— found the affair with my mother to his benefit. She, for her part, was not averse to sinning, since it provided her piety with new sustenance; for I have always noticed that the deity would find very few devoted among our race if people did not imagine him as a judge whose wrath they could forestall by voluntarily making confessions of an interesting nature. The state of inner conflict in which my mother now found herself sprang from the fact that she wanted not merely to be considered virtuous by others but also to appear virtuous to herself, while every day giving her weakness free rein. Had she been a resolute woman, she would at least have rescued the one or the other of her good qualities; yet since she was not such a woman, but rather one vacillating constantly between resolve and passion, all that was good in her eventually went to ruin, leaving nothing but a residue of selfishness and insufferability. I have encountered among my female acquaintances a good many such middling creatures, and it seems to me that this moral duplicity is the product of a female upbringing that unfortunately does not allow us to be open and honest.

And so my parents were opposites of a quite peculiar kind: my father complete unto himself, although in a manner I would not recommend; my mother very much incomplete and a veritable embryo in respect both to virtue and to vice. The two repelled each other as do like poles of a magnet, and that increased with the years. Were it not for my father's sense of delicacy, daily scandals would have ensued. No man had better refined the art of eluding his wife. Even when my mother was on the verge of breaking loose upon him like a storm, he would calm her with just a look or merely a word. I can truly say she never succeeded in venting her feelings upon him. There were times when she could have been choking with rage, but what good did it do? My father never gave her a chance to speak, and from the moment she had found a means of compensation in M——, my father was generous or considerate enough to pay little or no attention to what she did and to allow her all the more freedom, since he could be sure her lover would take every care to avoid public scandal.

I was the oldest of three children. My brother, Karl, exhibited from youth onward no special talents, and that is the reason why my father eventually favored me over the others. For no sooner had our lessons begun than it became evident that my lively interest was attracted by all possible things and that nothing of what can be taught and learned was too difficult for my mind. How often my father regretted that I had not turned out to be a boy—

and how often since then I came to regret it with him! Ninon d'Enclos was wont to say she had always prayed to God that he might make of her an honorable man rather than an honorable woman.[2] I do not know exactly what Ninon meant by that; but I definitely do know that had I been a man, I would also have been an honorable one; this I am assured by the strength of my temperament, which by nature tolerates no deceit and no betrayal. But now I am getting ahead of my story. I had barely reached the age of five when I had mastered reading and writing. At the age of seven I began to learn music, making such progress as to become widely admired. At this time my father began to teach me the art of deciphering; and however dull this art is, I became highly accomplished at it in a short time. My brain mass must be exceptionally soft and resilient; for every impression of my early years has remained, and however intricate and manifold my experiences have been, the years have still been unable to erase any of my memories completely. This is what now causes me my greatest suffering and what I have always strived but failed to destroy.

As a child I occupied the most unfortunate middle

[2] "Ninon d'Enclos" refers to Anne Lenclos (1620–1705), known as Ninon de Lenclos. She was a lady of fashion and courtesan known for her affairs with distinguished men as well as for her rebelliously libertine advocacy of the philosophies of skepticism and Epicureanism. She is the basis of the fictional figure Clarisse in Madeleine de Scudéry's novel *Clélie*.

ground between my mother and my father. More devoted to him than to her, I all too soon came to the point where I took sides against her whom I had to thank for giving me life. I believe it is a natural tendency that fathers, when they have sons, love their daughters more; yet I could not venture to give the reason for that. So too I believe that daughters love their fathers more than they do their mothers. For me this was absolutely the case. For my father I would have gone through the fires of Hell, as the saying goes; yet I was loath to do my mother even a small favor. Since I was by nature no more malicious than any other person, my unkindness may have been caused by the fact that as soon as my talents began to emerge, my mother wanted to play her role in my upbringing and as a rule imposed many a demand and restriction upon me. Because she held piety to be all-important, the first thing she did was to teach me several prayers. This I was willing to tolerate since poetry, and be it ever so bad poetry, is easy to learn if a person has a tolerable memory. I was less inclined to learn the so-called morality lessons. My liveliness was not at all compatible with the idea of sitting in half-dark rooms, as my mother loved to do. And it was still less compatible with being forced to sit still and endure boring conversation. So whenever it was possible I would evade my mother; and since a kind of instinct told me that this would not work without a certain degree of support from my father, I attached myself to him all the more. My father, it seems, was unable to resist. Perhaps he simply welcomed the diversion; perhaps he was misled by the wild notion that his spirit should deservedly live on in me. For whatever reason, from my ninth or tenth year on I was his decided favorite, and with that I then made rapid progress.

I must not forget to tell you that my brother and sister were neither a hindrance nor a help to me; I followed my own path entirely. If they got in my way, I would order them about with the authority peculiar to older siblings who have strength of will. I clearly recall that I mistreated my brother more than once, not because I did not like him but because I found his slow-wittedness irritating. My sister I treated just as if she were my little doll; sometimes I would dress her up, sometimes I would beat her. I took pleasure in making others tremble before me, and I began to take a liking to our neighbor's daughter because she always avoided me and on one occasion said to one of her playmates: That W—— girl is mean and nasty. All this is sufficient proof to me that despotism is part of our nature and that its opposite—whether we might call it humanity or love—is the product of a long process of adaptation and of the accurate estimation of the resistance we encounter in other people. I may be wrong, but I am very inclined to believe that by dint of the self-love that grows in each of us, people who are allowed to act despotically with impunity take pleasure in wielding that despotism and never with goodwill part with their accrued store of authority, however small it may be.

My contact with siblings and girlfriends ended the moment my father took me under his wing. We lived in the capital at a time of growing intellectual ferment, when the first foundations of a higher literature were being laid and pretensions to culture were a widespread concern. Translations from French and English prevailed until writers gradually began to try their own wings. Products of the mind then were different from those of today, but for that they gave no less pleasure. Voracious readers consumed everything that appeared. A new bookstore would open right next to an old one, since intellectual needs were arising that had to be satisfied. People then were still a long way from the intellectual factionalism prevalent among today's thinkers. The good minds sought out and supported each other, instead of isolating and persecuting each other the way they do so frequently nowadays. And what is more: the good minds were even sought out by those that were less so; people deemed themselves fortunate to spend a few hours in their company. And to the same degree that people today generally scorn those good minds, people then would try to lure them away from each other.

At that time nothing occupied the whole capital city more than the theater, and—as with all the new developments of those days—so too in the theater, where the public's taste had yet to be spoiled, people willingly made do with the homely fare available. Actors and actresses who today would gain no recognition were in those days deemed excellent and as much a delight to their audiences, male and female, as are the alleged master actors and actresses of today. The less people had thought about the rules of good taste, the more they enjoyed. People barely believed then that such rules existed; and no matter what the critics in our newspapers might say to the contrary, I am convinced that these rules exist only in their unfruitful minds and that the artists can do nothing worse than to take even the least notice of all that critical raving about art. The truth of the matter—at least it appears so to me—is that as art progresses, so too does criticism, and while criticism is a very superfluous thing, art remains indispensable. Can the most modern critics claim with even a grain of truthfulness that their abstract notions are the same as they were thirty years ago? Art is unknown territory, into which one must venture cautiously and without taking along a geographer as one's guide, for the whole of geography is of worth only after the discovery is complete. But where am I going with this? It is not yet the time for me to be taking flight from my story. At this early point in my life I am still free of vice; I have as yet incurred no guilt of which I would have cause to be ashamed.

My father loved drama and very frequently took me along to the theater when I was a ten-year-old girl. Most parents and teachers have no idea of the gradual development they went through themselves and thus assume that what they see or hear with no negative results can also be enjoyed by their children and pupils without harm. Without doubt my father was one of these thoughtless types. Yet when I look back upon my youth, I find that merely to have grown up into a tolerable person, I should better have not seen a play before I was eighteen or twenty. I am not able now to recount the first impressions drama made upon me; but I can say for sure that at first I found these impressions confusing. As soon as the first illusion had passed, I saw clearly that a person can be one thing and seem another; and for a young girl of ten or eleven like myself this abstract notion comes much too early; for I was yet to come to *be* something in order then to have a standard by which to measure what *seeming* was. But this was not the only harm I suffered from my many visits to the theater. The more agile my fantasy was by nature, the less did I fail to notice any of what I saw and heard on the stage. Not merely gestures and expressions but words and tones as well made such an indelible impression on my mind that the one play really would end for me only when I saw a new one. What I had liked on stage I would imitate at home. I declaimed monologues, and I would have given much indeed if I had found among my acquaintances a kindred spirit with whom I could have practiced dialogues. If I had been born twenty years later I would have had no trouble finding my like. But at the time I was developing, freethinking was not so widespread as it is now; people had not yet the vaguest idea of amateur theaters, the like of which we now encounter on almost every major street of the city. In the meantime I helped myself as well as I could. Whatever I was not able to act out by myself I left aside and turned with all the more zeal to practicing gestures. Even before I was eleven years old I had mastered the art of swooning so totally that I believe I could have competed with the best actress. I am naturally strong of temperament, and I do not recall ever in my life having felt the sense of weakness, caused when the blood drains back into the main vessels, that we call fainting or swooning; but I learned to copy this condition so well that I believe I deceived half the world. I experimented with this sort of thing more than once in order to foster my reputation as a woman of sentiment, and I succeeded so well that I had to laugh to myself afterwards about the naïveté with which certain people imagine we live and breathe only for their sake. My strong temperament was doubtless the reason that, like so many other young people, I far preferred tragedy to comedy. I have retained this preference, and when you finish reading my confessions you will have no trouble understanding why that is so. I note here only in passing that in my whole life I have laughed barely three times and that since my adolescence I have been so indifferent to this kind of emotion that I have far more often avoided than sought the opportunity to experience it. The actor's life I long deemed worthy of envy, and however often my father tried to persuade me of the opposite, I did not believe him until my closer acquaintance with persons of that type convinced me that, as a rule, they do not feel happy and that, deep down, they curse the craft they have chosen because it forces them to renounce their own individuality and makes them slaves to a public that can never be satisfied and that, even when it applauds, never relinquishes its right to scorn. The longer I took to become convinced of this truth, the longer I took to give up the idea of becoming an actress—for that thought hovered in the background of my soul for at least ten years and would always come to the fore whenever I felt I had irretrievably lost my reputation. And still I truly wish I had prevailed over all the difficulties that hindered my carrying out that thought! Whatever happened, I would have avoided all the collisions I had with my inclinations; whatever happened, I would have had greater unity of character; whatever happened, I would have had the greater freedom I needed and been able, if not to gain virtue, then at least to learn to avoid crime. I would not have become a happy person; but certainly, too, I would not have become a bad one.

Once my imagination had been sparked by drama, I then needed only to read novels as well, in order to make myself useless for life and its relationships once and for all. When Louis XV gave bonbons laced with cantharides to the women inhabiting the *Parc au Cerfs*, he knew what effect he wanted to call forth.[3] This is not the case with parents who let their daughters read novels; yet the effect of this kind of reading in most cases is just as certain as that of King Louis's candies and in its results even more terrible. Judging by my own experiences, I would forbid any young girl from reading a novel, no matter how good—that is, moral—it purports to be. For aside from the fact that such reading makes a habit of distraction by supplanting the taste for serious and useful activities, it also calls forth an indomitable inclination to adventurousness, which is all the more dangerous inasmuch as it is based upon the most dangerous of all passions, namely erotic love. My particular misfortune was to be born in times when people had no idea about all this and thus considered the reading of novels to be a necessity, in part because it cultivated the oral skills of young women—this mainly by teaching them phrases to memorize—and in

[3] Reference is to the Park-au-Cerf in Versailles, in the eighteenth century a backstreet locale for wayward, destitute girls. There King Louis XV sought out and seduced usually very young and poorly educated girls. This he is said to have done on occasion with the aid of candies laced with cantharides, a toxic preparation made from the crushed, dried bodies of the bright-green blister beetle (*Lytta vesicatoria* or *Cantharis vesicatoria*) of southern and central Europe. Commonly known in English as Spanish fly, it was formerly used as a counterirritant for skin blisters. Even since Roman times, it is believed to act as an aphrodisiac.

part because it enhanced the decorum of their behavior—this mainly by making them affectatious. My father himself brought me the novels that I was to read as soon as I had become devoted to this way of passing my time. Without doubt he thought he had done me a special favor when he provided me with a copy of Richardson's works; yet I can assure you that no book had a more adverse effect on me than did *Clarissa* and *Grandison*.[4] All the other novels had heated my blood, excited my fantasy, and put me in the mood to brood and ponder those mysteries I then felt compelled to fathom. *Clarissa* and *Grandison* diverted me from such pondering; but since the light that had been ignited in me remained, I could not fill my fantasy with gigantic figures without becoming confused and disoriented about all the rest of life. Grandison became my standard for men. Against him I measured all the men whose pleasing appearances caught my eye, especially those tall, well-built men whom, by dint of that instinct inborn in all women, I took to be the only ones worthy of notice. Since then I have done all within my power to desist from this foolish habit, but it has stayed with me against my will and had all too great an influence on my actions. Even today I seek that form of a man, as if hewn

[4] Samuel Richardson (1689–1761) was an English novelist who, while working on a manual for letter writing, completed *Pamela; or, Virtue Rewarded* (1739), considered the first modern English novel. It was followed by *Clarissa Harlowe* (1747–48) and *Sir Charles Grandison* (1753).

in the stone of Mt. Athos,[5] and even were the most perfect man in the world on earth to be mine, I would still be eternally tempted to treat him as I treated the one man whom fate did send me. I tell you again: Richardson's novels had the most adverse effect upon me, even if nature has not yet totally destroyed the form in which it has molded my character. Accordingly, she who is to take my place, if she is to turn out better than I did, must flee no other thing more than she flees those novels or their like. Once a misfortune has occurred, it cannot be made good again. The novels of Fielding, Smollett, and Goldsmith, which most people read with pleasure and with no real ill effect, did not appeal to me at all; they were all too confined by the boundaries of the possible to find my approval, and since I did not like to laugh, I was inclined to see the authors of *Tom Jones* and *Humphry Clinker* as harlequins whom one could not grow to like without rendering oneself profane. I want only to add that just as all things have their time, so too the interest *Clarissa* and *Grandison* awakened thirty years ago has passed and that had my formative years fallen in the times of the chivalric novels or even later, I would have become a completely different creature. That is the extent, I am convinced, to which the individual is bound by time and place.

---

[5] Mount Athos, located on a peninsula in Macedonian Greece, was considered since ancient times to be a holy place and has long been the center of Orthodox Christian monasteries.

I turn again to my mother. Never pleased with the education I was receiving from my father, she became still more displeased from the moment she lost her lover, who, if I am not mistaken, died when a case of indigestion resulted in a stroke. As soon as she had come to terms with her loss, she turned again to her family, in order to find in it some way of filling the gap that her loss had left in her life. She had always remained silent about my upbringing; but continuing to remain silent seemed to be beyond her powers, and that was all the more the case since I, having grown unaccustomed to dealing with her, looked upon her as a stranger and indeed also treated her as a stranger who held no rights over me. My mother's association with a clergyman had made her distrustful, with the result that she took my behavior to be the result of a conspiracy undertaken against her and instigated by my father. After attempting a few times and in vain to reconcile with him, she fell into a bitterness that, with my father feeling an insurmountable aversion towards her that could all too easily turn to deadly hatred, left her no other alternative but to immerse herself in loneliness. There then soon followed what usually happens with people of emotional temperament when events disrupt the course of their lives: she yielded to the pleasures of strong drink. From this moment on, her life was an unending succession of praying, drinking, and sleeping, and the more she accustomed herself to this way of living, the more she preferred her loneliness. Not that she would not now and then have called me or my brother or sister to her; but all in all we mattered as little to her as did the rest of the world; she was living for another world, growing all the more afire with enthusiasm, the closer she came to her goal. It is strange how our desires turn more and more towards the infinite, the more we stray from our true calling. But it probably must be so if anything great is to become of our human race, and I have often thought that even if our belief in the hereafter were to have no other cause than this infinity of our desires, the destruction of that faith would still be regrettable, as I imagine that perfect sensibility and reason would bring with them a great deal of stagnation.

I had reached the age of about thirteen when my desire to know all about certain mysteries reached an intensity that left me no rest. My father evaded all the questions I posed to him in this matter. I turned to our cook, a woman of rather advanced years; yet as obliging as such people may be, as long as it was only a matter of satisfying my curiosity, I was able to press no more out of her than the answer that I would learn everything in due time. My father's manservant was a dullard and so ugly as well that I could never look at him without revulsion. Left to my own devices, I brooded incessantly until, through heaven knows what combination of notions, I hit upon the right means.

Not far from our house was a boarding school in which a French count—a man who had been compelled to flee his fatherland as the result of a duel—taught lessons in his mother tongue. Every day I would watch the count pass by my window, and the arrogance with which he strode along had long since captured my attention as much as had his truly handsome figure. To meet with his pleasure I had made the acquaintance of several young ladies from the school, albeit without in any way furthering the success of my goal. As soon as I saw that I would achieve my intentions only if I could be alone with the count, I asked my father's permission to continue my study of French, a pursuit I had begun more than once before but had then always abandoned. This permission I was not denied, and since one does not like to return to a master whom one has previously dismissed, it was understood that Count Vaudreuil would be my teacher.[6] He came to my house as summoned. My father was present for the first lessons; but restless as he always was, he soon wearied of presiding in this fashion. Vaudreuil was all too

[6]Throughout her confessions, the narrator draws comparisons between her own experiences and those of great ladies of the courts of King Louis XIV, XV, and XVI. The name of her first lover evokes this sphere as well, belonging to a sequence of marquises and counts who played a significant role above all in the French colonizing of the New World. A Louis Philippe de Rigaud, comte de Vaudreuil, took part in the American war of independence and was decorated in 1789 by Louis XVI. He emigrated in 1792 and returned to France under the consulate.

much the Frenchman and too ashamed of his profession not to take advantage of the opportunity that my father had thus offered him to become involved in a love affair. A lover has an all the better time of it when his beloved is burning with impatience for him to reveal certain mysteries to her; and since this was all too much the case with me, I accepted his caresses with all the more open eagerness. Vaudreuil postponed the consummation of our affair, without my being able at that time to understand his reason for doing so; he was preparing me for the moment in every possible way, and later I saw quite clearly that he counted among the roués of his day who liked to enjoy none but the most exquisitely prepared love. It would be disgusting if I were to recount here the stages he led me through; but I must not leave unsaid that he gradually instilled in me a raging passion that left me no choice but to ask, as if for a favor, that he render me the ultimate step, the coup de grâce of our affair. This was doubtless the point to which he wanted to bring me, for the self-love of French people from society's higher circles is, in the truest sense of the word, immeasurable, and the greatest sacrifice one renders them ceases to be a sacrifice if it is not bound up with the total prostitution of one's self. Vaudreuil achieved this goal with me. Boundless was the love I felt for him. He could have tyrannized me, and I still would have continued to caress him. To such an extent I had lost my bearings, the guiding tramontane of my life's voyage, that I pursued him wherever he went.[7] I felt as if my entire life hung on his every breath. A long-repressed fire had finally broken out, and it flared up in proportion to the rich fuel it received.

If I have said nothing until now about my figure, that is simply because it was still developing at this time. At about fourteen years old, I had reached the same height I am now, that is: taller than average. My face was round in shape. In my eye, which one must imagine to be fiery, there was a certain glint of triumph; only later on did it take on a definite downward direction, towards the ground, and I shall not forget to indicate at what time it first assumed this direction. My coloring had the freshness of youth, with that extra something that comes with being a brunette. I was not fleshy, but I did have the disposition to become so. Faced with these charms, German men would have been pleased to be in Vaudreuil's place; but Vaudreuil was all the less so, since people were so obliging to him at every opportunity as to turn him to favor self-love above any other kind. Whatever I might

---

[7] In the German, the narrator claims that her attraction to Vaudreuil caused her to "lose her tramontane." The phrase is a direct translation of the Italian *perdere la tramontana* ("to lose one's bearings"). "Tramontane," the classical term for a northern wind, refers to the northern or northeasterly wind sweeping down from the Alps and Appenines to the west coast of Italy. It is valued by Italian fishermen and sailors of old as a swift guide out to sea. The phrase recurs later in the narrative, and in both cases it suggests that the narrator's intense emotions left her bereft of the usual guiding forces in her life, setting her adrift and out of control.

try in order to captivate him, there always remained fixed between us a certain gulf, of which I was very clearly aware but which I could never explain. One day I saw he was irritated, and I sought the reason for his ill humor until I learned he was in need of money. What could I do? I had nothing myself; and since all my needs, indeed even my fantasies, were satisfied, I also had never experienced any wish to possess things. Yet now I would have liked to have all the treasures of Peru to lay at my lover's feet. I pondered this way and that how I might ease his embarrassment, until I hit upon the easiest means. What more need I say? I stole a considerable sum from my father and gave it to my lover, who took it without a second thought. One should have thought he would now at least have begun to reward my devotion. But he did nothing of the sort. His easy manner remained as it had been before. Gratitude was something of which he seemed to have no conception, and if he did not leave me at once, it was not likely for any other reason than that he took pleasure in having in me a ready thief.

This all happened in the short time of a month and a half. Is it possible to go more to ruin in a shorter time than I did? I myself had no idea about that, and I would have gone on giving myself over to my passion for Vaudreuil, had not my father noticed the deficit I had caused in his cash holdings. Money has a binding or dividing power, according to the circumstances. My passion for Vaudreuil could not have escaped my father's attention, since it had changed my entire being; but he had not considered taking notice, since it was of no disturbance to him. After he discovered the theft, his attitude changed. He called me to account about it, and since I did not deny in the least that I had taken the money and admitted to him as well that Vaudreuil had received it and promised to pay it back, he put an end to the entire matter by writing a letter to my language teacher, informing him that he might concern himself with me no longer, since it was his intention that I accompany my father on his pending travels. That latter point he announced to me as well, and whether he meant it seriously or not, I still had no time to lose. Every day I had to see my Vaudreuil at least once, to say nothing of the countless letters I wrote to him, in which, with all the truthfulness born of passion and all the nonsense born of madness, I lamented the harsh blows of fate.

We held our trysts in a remote garden where Vaudreuil had rented a room. It was a lovely spring day. Arm in arm we were walking up and down a lane of cherry trees in bloom, when Vaudreuil inquired about certain phenomena, the periodic recurrence of which is so decisive for the good name of unmarried women. I did not understand him at first; but when he explained himself more clearly, I was forthright enough to admit to him that these symptoms had disappeared since I had begun keeping company with him. He was taken aback, and how that could happen to a man of his character I understand even less today than I did then; but his color changed so markedly that I became anxious and asked if something was wrong.

"Nothing, nothing," he answered, "I was just thinking that I did not want to make you unhappy; the world is so foolish, and a young girl in your situation does not have the right to defy this foolish world. You are coming to see me again tomorrow. Good!— I shall give you a bottle that you must drink down in one gulp. You will have to do that while I am watching to make sure you do not become too frightened to do it."

I found this all confusing and strange; but before I had time to think about it, Vaudreuil changed the subject. He became more cheerful than I had ever seen him before, and with his giving me one proof after another of his love, I completely forgot what we had been talking about and, when the hour of our parting came, left him more reluctantly than ever.

The next day, Vaudreuil did not give me the bottle until a few minutes before we parted.

"It's all for the best," he said. I stared at him.

"It's for your own good," he repeated.

"And even if you are poisoning me, Vaudreuil," I said, "I shall still empty this bottle, trusting you fully."— I lifted the bottle to my lips. The medicinal smell was repulsive, a distillate of all Hell itself. But no matter, I drank it to the last drop. Vaudreuil had obviously noticed how badly I suddenly began to feel, and he took me in his strong arms and bore me out to the carriage waiting outside the garden gate.

"Take her home as quickly as possible," he called to the coachman, who spared not a moment, for in a few minutes I was there. I felt strange. By and by I felt a weariness that made it impossible for me to stay on my feet. That weariness I then felt give way to a fearsome uproar in my blood. Then cramps began that I thought would cost me my life. I was seized by a series of dreadful evacuations, and Vaudreuil's goal was achieved at last.

For several days, I thought I was about to die. The doctors called in made suspicious faces and prescribed their traditional and conventional remedies. I was smart enough to take none of them, since I had not been able to make any sense of my affliction. My sound constitution was enough to pull me through, and my indescribable exhaustion gave way to an irresistible weariness. Then, after I had slept for twenty-four straight hours, I felt for certain I would recover. And from then on I yearned for the moment that would restore Vaudreuil to me again.

This moment came after about twelve days, which I needed to recover my full strength. I hurried to the garden where I was accustomed to meet Vaudreuil and made ready to reprimand him for showing me no sign of life during that long time; but there, upon inquiring after him, I was given a letter that read as follows:

> I have left the capital to return to my fatherland. I would have liked to have waited for you to recover, but that was impossible for a thousand reasons. I cannot part from you completely without telling you that a love such as the one you feel is out of place in our times. See to it now that you find a husband, or you are lost. Adieu.

Imagine a fourteen-year-old girl so unkindly betrayed, and you will find it forgivable that I saw in Vaudreuil one of those monsters who do their dastardly deeds in *Clarissa* and *Grandison*. I walked a few more times up and down the garden walkways, and as I left the garden, I could not suppress a stream of tears. I had a hard time drying my eyes when I came through the city gate; but once I had told myself that that disloyal man would not be returning, I also summoned the courage to forget him. And thus did I return to my father's house.

I had been through experiences that could have set my life upon a different path, had my fate been more favorable. My father's plans to travel came to naught; all the arrangements were complete, when the arrival of a letter, whose contents I was never able to learn, decreed that we should stay home. At no other time did I see my father more introspective than he was then; it was as if he were brooding over a single thought that, though it was supposed to give rise to some resolve, simply would not do so. My mother's condition grew worse day by day, and while I did indeed visit her, I did so far more out of curiosity than for any other reason; I found it interesting to observe what progress she was making towards her ultimate demise. Except for my brother and sister, who, touched by nothing, lived out their days in youthful abandon, our entire family was in a fearful state of crisis that had to be resolved sooner or later.

No state is more conducive to poetry than that of dissatisfaction with one's self and one's entire environment. One creates an ideal world if one is unhappy in the real world. This is so much a part of human nature that I now understand full well how the mood in which I now found myself not only made poetic works more appealing to me than they had been before but also imparted to me even to this day a poetic power of my own. You are acquainted with Wieland's early works.[8] From them my spirit took most of its nourishment, and by learning them almost by heart I laid the foundation for the religious zeal that, as I shall soon relate to you, proved one of my positive traits

[8] Christoph Martin Wieland (1733–1813) was the son of a Swabian pastor of strongly Pietistic leanings. Young Wieland was much influenced by essential ideas of that movement in seventeenth- and eighteenth-century Protestantism against rigid dogma and orthodoxy and in favor of subjectivity felt religion, and his early poetry expresses that struggle against French and English rationalism. In 1752 he was called to Zurich by the Swiss poet and critic J. J. Bodmer and, with Klopstock and Bodmer, produced works of a religious-sentimental nature such as *Sympathien* (1755; "Sympathies") and *Empfindungen eines Christen* (1757; "Sentiments of a Christian").

and served, as it were, as a guiding aegis to my tendency to excess. Klopstock's *Messiah*, the first songs of which had appeared, I found still more exalting.[9] Without having had the least tutelage in the art of prosody, I had no trouble deducing its rules, and once in possession of them I took the greatest pleasure in pressing all my thoughts into poetic form—an activity in which I soon became so adept that for some time I was able to write only in verse and thanks to which people always took pleasure in hearing me speak. Of my works I shall tell you nothing. I burned them, and I believe I was not wrong to have done so, although I am convinced they had just as much worth as the boneless stuff they sell to us nowadays as poetry.

Five or six months passed amid such pursuits. Of Vaudreuil I thought only in those moments when my long-betrayed sensuality asserted itself—moments that in my present state were as seldom as they were fleeting. Had I been given any lasting encouragement, I would have been, mere female that I was, a poetess; but it was my fate that none of my qualities were to develop fully. As the crisis of which I was just telling was passing, I underwent a transformation that I shall describe to you as thoroughly as I am able.

---

[9] Friedrich Gottlieb Klopstock (1724–1803) published in 1748 the first hymns of his massive *Messias*, a work revolutionary in its image of the poet as exalted, sublime visionary, voicing his religious insights and feelings in free, rhapsodic verse.

I knew that my mother could not go on living much longer, and I was braced for her death without actually wishing she would die; for as she was no longer a hindrance to me, she counted among those people for whom we feel neither love nor hatred and whom we see go on living or perishing without experiencing joy or sorrow either way. The filth in which she was living had made her so repulsive to me that I no longer went to see her; but since I did not think of her either, she was as good as not there at all for me. For some time now my father had given her completely free rein in her love of strong drink and adopted no other tactic than . . . a progressive strengthening of those drinks. Her end was in sight but not to be foretold as to day or hour. Her temperament put up an unbelievable resistance. Without noticing the treacherous strategy by which her life was being shortened, she spoke only of the kind benevolence of her husband, and, thus made doubly blissful by drink and affection, she gave no thought at all to her approaching death, until one afternoon she felt a stabbing pain rend her deep within and set the entire house in upheaval with her screams. Called to her bedside, I was witness to the inexpressible torment she suffered. Since I did not know what I was to make of it all, I sent for my father, who was in the neighborhood. He sent word back to me that he could not come and that the cramps would soon pass, adding that we should not cause a fuss and not send for a doctor until he arrived home. What was I to do? Watching my mother lying there, seized by the most violent convulsions, her bluish lips frothing—that was all the more unbearable for me the longer it went on, and as I was feeling much too acutely the difference between the idea of tragedy and real tragedy, I went back to my room, incapable of any other activity, but still by far not as restless as thousands upon thousands of other daughters would have been in my position. After some hours, I was brought word that my mother had died. I received this news without the slightest show of emotion, and when my father arrived home at that very same moment, I needed only to gaze into his calm face to know that no affectation of grief was required of me. He was doubtless making a sacrifice to propriety by resolving to go look at her corpse. I accompanied him into my mother's bedroom. He was taken aback to see her lying there, her features completely changed; but he said not a word and returned to his room after the first minute. On the following day the funeral arrangements were made, and on the day after that, towards evening, she was quietly laid to rest, and barely eight to twelve days had then gone by when there was no more talk at all of my mother; since no pleasant recollections brought her image to our minds, she was simply forgotten, just as we tend to forget a pain we have withstood.

What happened after these events is that my father became indisposed and was confined to his sofa. It was not anything serious, and he himself ascribed it to the disgust that the sight of my dead mother had caused him. Since over the years he had become accustomed to constant diversion, this confinement caused him to become, at best, grumpy. My brother and sister were still too young to be able to cheer him; instead, they disturbed him to such a degree that he preferred more to see them departing than arriving. Under these circumstances I, whom he had always held dear, now became a necessity for him, and thus all the dearer. Through my association with Vaudreuil I had learned the art of affecting moods, and while practicing this art upon my unwell father I took such pleasure in my behavior that I had to be pleasing him more by far. I sought out every means I knew to dispel his boredom. Among other things I confided in him my efforts at poetry. He grew eager to see some of them. I read to him the ones I considered the best. He was astonished at my talent and urged me to cultivate it. All this while he was even more pleased with the attentiveness with which I anticipated his every need or wish. It was as if totally new feelings were awakening in him. Time and again he pressed my hand. My father, as much as any other man, had carefully cultivated his personality all his life. Yet he lost that composure completely when he encountered a daughter who was the very embodiment of devotion. He began to confide in me; he told me of the ways and means by which he had come to win my mother and how he had been able to live neither with nor without her, until her love of drink had spoiled her for him completely. It was a very ordinary marital tale but, coming from my father, it meant a great deal: he, who kept everything to himself, had confided in me.

He was still telling me this story when a stranger came to visit, demanding some document or other that he had entrusted to my father. Since my father's condition did not permit him to leave the sofa without experiencing discomfort, he handed me the key to his desk with the request that I fetch the required document. Without so much as a second thought, I took the key. The paper was nowhere to be found. But while I was rummaging through everything, I came upon a box that had written on it in large letters: "Poison"! I cannot tell you what a powerful impression these few letters made upon me: I lost my senses so completely that I stood there as if petrified, my motionlessness making it necessary for my father, despite all his pain, to rise from the sofa and come to help me. He found the document at once; but when he saw my eyes fixed motionless on the box, he understood at once why I was so astonished. Hastily he dispatched the stranger in order to avoid a scene that could have meant danger for him. Then he attempted to assume an air of unwitting innocence and take up his story where he had had to break it off; but when he kept faltering despite this resolve and I sat looking at him with a gaze that foretold questions he could have no great desire to answer, he replied briefly, saying:

"I see what you're thinking: your question cannot be answered with a few words. I shall tell you at the right time about what you must know."

This was only half a confession, but I took it to be a full one. Since my father at that moment was the only human being I loved, I made every conceivable effort at least to excuse him—if not to justify him—for committing such a terrible act as poisoning seemed to me at that time. I thought back to the state in which my mother had been for years—to her vices, to her disgusting condition, to her uselessness in society, to the inevitability of her death. On this last point I told myself that her death would have come in two, at most three months, and in this way I succeeded in not hating my father. But what an immeasurable gulf lies between not hating and trust! How was I to bridge that gulf? I cursed the moment that I made the fatal discovery. Like a great stone the secret of the poisoning weighed upon my breast; it bore down all the heavier upon me since this was the first secret I had to keep and since I had to admit that I myself had brought it to light. I do not know whether magnanimity is habitual to certain privileged souls, but I have always found that it presupposes an unpleasant situation. More than once I asked myself whether it was not my duty to inform the legal authorities regarding the sudden death of my mother and my suspicions about it. And if I have understood myself correctly, I did this only as a way of convincing myself indirectly and secretly that my father's life—or at least his freedom—was in my hands. I confess that such feelings always struck me as alien and strange in every way; but what was fitting or not for my poetic world was in no way connected with what I felt was necessary for the real world; and if there had been some external incitement for me to betray my father, I would have feigned resistance at first but surely then would have succumbed to it very quickly.

You will be so kind as to recall that I had been occupying myself with poetry for several months and that everything that occurred in my parents' house during that time necessarily must have played a role in giving me what philosophers call "intension," in imparting essentials of my character.[10] Bearing that in mind, you can easily understand that I could not have been confirmed at a more

---

[10] The German asserts simply that parental homelife necessarily gave the narrator what philosophers call intension. While at first glance perhaps a misspelling or typographical error, *intension* (not *intention*) is a term from philosophical language still used in both languages. It occurs in and since the writings of Kant and Leibniz and, in this explicitly philosophical context, means "basic essential meaning," the essential characteristics of a concept or term. The translation retains the original's reference to philosophers but adds the phrase "in imparting essentials of my character" to indicate how the narrator's experiences in the parental household did much to shape her personality. Her use of the term speaks further to her more than superficial awareness of the philosophical discourse of her day.

opportune time. The clergyman who performed this office was considered to be the most honest and enlightened man of his profession. I presented myself to him with as much innocence as I was able to summon up, and I had the good fortune to be taken for what I was presenting myself to be. A quickness to learn is the first requisite of every future penitent, and I showed no lack of it. But along the way I became bored with the process of indoctrination, and as a certain amount of coquetry began to play a role in the proceedings, I began to come up with objections for which the good man was not prepared. To excuse my behavior I said that I had read a good deal and that when I expressed doubts that did not originate in my own mind, I was doing it so that such doubts would no longer torment me. Using this fine excuse, I took advantage of every possible opening. My objections were refuted, whereupon I would affect a look meant to convey my conviction that there was no refuting the argument the good cleric had put forward. To win him over even more, I would enliven his lectures, which in the course of time had become somewhat lame, by mixing in my feelings, and this would soften his heart all the more, the more foreign to him those feelings were. But what completely enchanted him was the fact that I never let a single word of his presentation go by unnoticed. Proof of that I gave him by presenting, at the start of each new lesson he taught me, a recapitulation of the previous one, and indeed as complete a summary as he could possibly have wished. Since my receptivity was in fact quite comprehensive and since I had little or no trouble writing, I did not find this work at all difficult, and what I gained by it was totally out of proportion with the little time I spent on it. For it occurred to me that my confirmator was an excellent tool for creating a certain reputation for myself. By praising my talents he praised me in general; and what praise could I have preferred to that of a clergyman whose impartiality was part and parcel of his office? Without doubt, I was deceiving him by acting this way; but there are circumstances in which deception is unavoidable. I myself was far from understanding my actions. In such a wondrous way did I mix religiosity with vanity and with my drive to acquire a reputation that I did not know which played the primary role. I carried things still further as my confirmation process approached its goal. In addition to the recapitulations of the lessons, I also brought my confirmator prayers and monologues that, given the manner in which I had composed them—that is, according to the value people in those days were wont to accord sonorous phrases—had to be considered pure masterpieces and in fact were declared to be such by my confirmator. I finished by composing a proper confession of faith that I had no sooner presented than it was propounded by all the faithful souls of the parish to be a model of edification that merited being presented to all young girls my age. My act of confirmation I shall pass over in silence in order that I might not have to comment on the ostentatious splendor with which people poison the most sacred rites. Many had been invited to attend; whatever modesty was still in me was lost on this day amid all the praise rained down upon me; I realized clearly in that moment that a person could deceive and reap great thanks for the deception. Pride and joy radiated from the eyes and features of my confirmator. I clung to what humility I needed for the moment; yet I left the company fully convinced that I had perpetrated a hoax, and I returned home as exhausted as any actress who had spent several hours on end offering herself up as a sacrifice to her public. Within mere days, the entire course of religious study I had gone through sank from memory within me and only those consequences remained that resulted from the acquaintance I had made with the family of my confirmator.

Before I tell of these events, I must return to my father. Doing so, I shall speak of things that, since they occur only rarely, people tend to declare to be impossible. I do not like to tell of these matters; but having resolved to write my confessions, I want to write them all, without letting myself be misled by some notion of shame. My father, then, had noted the change in my attitudes as they related to himself far too well to leave me at the point that I had reached after my association with Vaudreuil. The fear that drove him was intensified in no small measure by the visits that my confirmator made to him when he was instructing me in the teachings of Christianity. The more that good man spoke of me in such tones of praise, and the more extensively he gave vent to his feelings about my delicate sense of morality, the more worried my father became that in a moment of weakness I might bring forth a confession, my eternal silence on which meant everything to him. In order to prevent this he could find no better means than to instill in me an entirely new kind of interest in himself. How he was able to bring himself to do this, I cannot say; but I do know that a young girl's sensuality, once aroused, makes her susceptible to the seductive powers of the entire male gender. At least that was how it was in my case. My father began by giving several expensive gifts. These would have sufficed to make me vow eternal silence, had he believed they were enough. Upon gifts followed caresses—at first verbal ones, then real ones. I was ashamed for my father's soul, but I had lost the right to be ashamed for my own. Accordingly, the resistance I offered was but half a resistance, so that all that was needed was a serious assault to bring me down. And such an assault was not long in coming; for my father, who clearly saw that people with whom no virtuous relationship was possible could be won over by vice, descended upon me one night and, pleading in one moment, using force in the next, made me his bedfellow. To assuage my conscience he repeated his blandishments; but to make his success more complete he spoke of all morality as a restraining leash for those who had a need to be deceived. Thus at that moment I was a du Barry whenever I was proclaimed a model of piety and virtue;[11] but I confess honestly that precisely this situation contributed in no small way to sustaining my interest in morality. The contradiction between my actions and the prevailing rules meant to guide them gave me all the more pleasure, since I was able to tell myself: Where there is no law, there is also no sin. However things may stand with morality, I said to myself, by rights it cannot mean anything to me until they have run their course. And so I tolerated my father's embraces out of the spirit of defiance that one finds to some degree, according to their nature, in all people. Even the savage at times seeks pleasure in desecrating, for the sake of change, the deity he usually worships. Can a person who has no fear worship anything but herself?— But let me turn from these reflections back to my confessions.

Since you were born and raised in the capital, you will know the R—— family, at least by reputation. It was the family of my confirmator, who, in his loyalty, did not rest

[11] The "de Berri" in the original refers to Madame du Barry, Marie Jeanne Bécu (1743–93), who in 1768 succeeded Madame Pompadour as the mistress of King Louis XV until his death in 1774. She dominated both king and court, becoming famous for her prodigality as a patron of artists and men of letters.

until he had introduced me to them. If it was his intention in doing so to offer me to them as a model of virtue, he was making a mistake; if he believed that his daughters, through their example, could make flourish and grow in me the seeds of the proper attitudes that he had planted in me, then he was more wrong still. I am not saying this to cast a shadow on this man's good judgment; but I maintain that any cleric, the way things stand now, must be confused about how people are and that there is nothing left for him to do but withdraw with a certain show of good nature. He had no fewer than five daughters; but as different as they may have been from each other, there was not a single one of them who was a shade better than I. Very soon I noticed that what their father took into such high account in me had little value in their eyes. This, by their way of thinking, was quite another matter, which, though it might cast a favorable light on my talents, had nothing at all to do with my other qualities and which would cause me no harm or hindrance to do without. This judgment was most clearly evident from the reception they accorded me—which, by the way, gave me sufficient evidence that nothing had become known of my association with Vaudreuil, for indeed they treated me like a neophyte whose eyes they would have to open. The occasion for that was all too soon in coming.

Their father was just about to accompany me, when our lesson had ended, out of the house when, as we were coming through the parlor door, we saw an artillery officer descending the stairs. The old man was so taken aback by this sight that he, though in fact not a small man, seemed to grow a full span in height. It was the most unpleasant incident possible, and Father R—— clearly saw it as a threat to the good name of his daughters. Fortunately the young man he had just caught was not lacking presence of mind. Before the shocked father could utter a word, the artillery officer, with a show of utmost respect, spoke as follows: "I am looking for one of my friends; they direct me to this house; lost in thought, I walk up the stairs and come upon a family who, fortunately, are able to tell me I want the next house over." This simple tale calmed the good old man at once. How was he to respond? Was not the man who had just excused himself in this manner wearing a sword? I have always noted that this implement, so innocent and harmless in times of peace, invests those who wear one with more credibility than they deserve. I myself had not a moment's doubt as to what I should think of the incident, and I took the matter for what it really was, namely for a revelation about my new friends.

They had not failed to notice that I was present when the young man was caught. On the very same day, the youngest of them visited me and, without my soliciting her as a confidante, told me what an embarrassing situation her sister Minnie—her second oldest sister—could have been in. I took care not to say a single word—good or bad—about that. When she talked about how strict her father was, I took up the cause of all fathers, but without exactly condemning the daughters. About my own father, I told her, I never had any cause to complain; since he knew my inclinations, he placed his trust in me; no girl could have more freedom than I did.

"But still you keep on studying?" Caroline asked.

"What else am I supposed to spend my time doing?" was my answer. "I have no other company than yours, and you yourself know how seldom I enjoy that."

And as one word led to another in this manner, I learned that each of my new friends had her own suitor, whom she was seeing both in and outside of the parental home. With that we went and sat at the window, and barely half an hour had gone by when an aspiring young junior lawyer came by to draw Caroline into a conversation. I withdrew circumspectly so as not to hinder their free exchange of ideas, but doing so, I was only half successful in making Caroline beholden to me, as her aim had been no less than to summon her lover, and she saw clearly that she could not dare to do so now.

By and by I came to know the affairs of the other sisters; yet no matter how much trouble they took to make me a party to their interests, I still followed the same tactics with them that I had initiated with Caroline. I acquired early on a clear idea of prevailing necessities. Even though I had acquired a good reputation on the strength of qualities upon which I placed little value, I still understood very clearly that I could maintain that reputation only by dint of those same qualities. Even the most minor denial of the R—— family on my part would have meant my irreparable ruin. I kept this fact in mind constantly to guide the way I behaved towards them. My most difficult task in doing this was preventing my house from being made into a general trysting place for their rendezvous. They themselves made that their main goal, for from time to time they would allow their suitors to surprise them in my rooms, hoping to make me accustomed to the practice. But I had no sooner taken note of their true intentions than I gave them such pointed signals about my father's strictness regarding matters of good reputation that they no longer dared to arrange encounters in my house. And then, once I had been initiated into their secrets, they could not break off their friendship with me without facing considerable risk; yet I, on the other hand, could withdraw from the relationship at any time—and even do so with a look of triumph whenever I chose to enjoy that victory.

In order to play my role all the better, I continued, even after the confirmation was over, to maintain my relationship to old R——; and not satisfied even with that, I took up with all the old ladies whose acquaintance I made in his home. This segment of human society is all the more receptive to the attentiveness one shows it, the more it is generally neglected and slighted; yet since it never ceases to have a place and voice in society, a good relationship to it is for all young persons, be they of male or female gender, of utmost importance. Striking was the fact that I told myself this at even less than sixteen years of age; but was not such an insight directly linked to the relationship I had to the young R—— daughters? Those who attribute such insights to instinct may on that point have an account to settle with sound human reason. In my case I believe we expect too much of instinct if we attribute to it all the clever insights a young girl can have when she understands her situation clearly. The faction with which I had taken up was indeed the best I could have chosen. The old ladies repaid the interest I showed in them by drawing me into their circle; and by treating all others with the same solicitous attitude that I showed them, I won favor on all sides and in short order created for myself a circle of acquaintances that was much to my credit and that, in all manner of diverse ways, compensated for the boredom inseparably bound up with such behavior.

While in this manner I was at work, with a cunning that is surely quite rare in someone my age, to make myself widely proclaimed as a young person of the most brilliant intellect and best manners, the relationship in which I had been living with my father continued. Often in life I have repeated to myself those words of Shakespeare:

"Who would 'scape the birch if merit should decide?"[12] Of all the people I knew, not a single one had any idea how matters really stood with me; and who should have suspected such a thing, since there was no way of knowing I had begun where others drew the line? The deeper I was mired in transgression, the more sure of myself I was; people looked at me as if I were a saint. What would have been the result if by some chance people had seen the du Barry in me? I even posed this question to myself

[12] The passage that the narrator purports to quote here occurs in act 2, scene 2, of *Hamlet*, where the original English wording is, "use every man / after his desert, and who should 'scape whipping?" (Shakespeare, *Complete Works* 2: 612). The English offered here, instead of giving Shakespeare's original, adheres closely to the narrator's German quotation in order to highlight her version's difference both from Shakespeare and from August Wilhelm Schlegel's translation of *Hamlet*, which, having appeared, to great and lasting acclaim, in Berlin in 1798 and likewise published by Unger, was surely known to the author and readers of the *Confessions*. Schlegel stays very close to the original: "Behandelt jeden Menschen nach seinem Verdienst, und wer ist vor Schlägen sicher?" (*Hamlet* 67). In contrast, the German quoted by the narrator reads, "Wer würde dem Staubbesen entrinnen, wenn das Verdienst entscheiden sollte?" By rendering Shakespeare's "whipping" with the implement used (*Staubbesen*, a then common variation of *Staupbesen*, the bundle of birch rods used for corporal punishment, usually judicial), the narrator's version harks back to the mid-1760s *Hamlet* translation by Wieland, in its revised form by Johann Joachim Eschenburg long the most widely read German *Hamlet* and also the basis for the most popularly staged version of that time, by Friedrich Ludwig Schröder. This echo of the Wieland-Eschenburg-Schröder tradition reflects the female narrator's participation in the reading mania and theater enthusiasm of her day. The conspicuous neglect of the Unger house's own much-lauded *Hamlet* translation by Schlegel might also be traced back to various rifts between the Schlegels and the Unger publishing house after 1801.

on more than one occasion when fate was bearing me so high; and still it did not make me uneasy. Who could betray me? In the young men as well I could see the respect felt for me; for with me they lost the frivolous tone with which they campaigned for the favors of other beauties; they considered me one of those to be won over with deliberate and proper care, and they spoke to me in solemn tones, which I suffered quite gladly, because my self-esteem was most richly compensated for the self-denial it all cost me.

What was going on between me and my father could in the meantime not but become tedious for us. This relationship came to an end from the moment I made it clear to my father that I had seen through his intentions and that his secret was kept as safe as could be in my breast. With the R—— family I remained, as they say, on good terms, by continuing, without becoming in the least bit arrogant about the good fortune I had made in the world, to confide in my former confirmator and current confessor certain minor matters that, on the assumption they are the only ones a person has to confide, are always well received and that also gave me a position against his daughters that prevented them from crossing the line I had drawn. I would have felt happy, were it not that we tend to take things for granted. My activity in these circles was not without its entertaining moments; but it lacked one certain goal, even though there were prospects of a brilliant marriage. A so-called *affaire de cœur* was what I was missing, but how was I to bring one about? The greatest care was in order lest I tear down in one moment all I had taken such trouble to achieve. I feared the men on account of their inconstancy; but this fear was not my greatest; for I trembled more by far at the prospect of their garrulousness, which seemed to me all the more likely a danger, since I had built a reputation of being a rational person who could not be conquered in one onslaught, or in other words: since a triumph over me appeared to be a genuine triumph about which one would be loath to remain silent. I did not know how I was to find my way out of the contradiction that I had created for myself, when, quite unexpectedly, Lieutenant von P—— declared his love to me.

He had encountered me quite frequently at social gatherings and clearly found it worth the trouble to see how much of my outward look of virtuous behavior was mere appearance and how much of it was truth. Those who knew this particular man so favored by others of my gender will recall that he was never at a loss for some object of his affections and also how hard it was to resist him. As soon as he deemed me worthy of his special attention, I took all the more firm a grip on myself the more I feared some kind of secret arrangement could be at the bottom of it. Without rejecting him, I gave no reason for him to nurture any kind of hope. In this way, I kept him at a distance for some time. The gifts he sent me I did accept, without asking from whom they came; I even wore them, since I was able to assume he would be particularly pleased to see me do so. At last letters arrived bearing his signature. These I left unanswered for two reasons: for one, because I knew he had not written them himself, since he could not write much more than his own name; for another, because I could not be sure that my writing would not be misused, allowing that should he be only mildly interested in me personally, a letter from me would easily pass from one hand to another until it arrived at a place where it could ruin my reputation. I note here in passing that I had observed this policy since my involvement with Vaudreuil, and I was pleased to have done so; at the same time I confess that I came to find nothing as difficult as remaining true to this maxim, since I was always plagued by my love of aesthetic pursuits. In the meantime, Herr von P—— did not cease presenting himself to me, and his self-assurance grew when he saw me wearing his favors. As I was pleased with his colossal build and handsome face, I also reckoned to my favor the fact that he, as a nobleman, would be less inclined to betray me if I were successful in instilling in him a more than casual interest in me. I had decided to yield to his pleas, yet not determined the manner of doing so. To enter into a serious love story with an experienced man was ridiculous. Nevertheless I had to instill in him the idea that he was the first to triumph over my virtue, because otherwise he could be tempted to speak of me as a hypocrite. To prevent this from happening, I maintained my chasteness the whole time. Amid a stream of tears I accepted his declarations.

"I am in your hands," I said to him, "but you will treat me magnanimously; how could you make an innocent girl unhappy?"

Such phrases were not for Herr von P——, and so I changed what I was saying, only that I continued to play coy and naive. Every serious advance I met with most resolute resistance. The various rendezvous proposed to me I took greatest care to avoid, because I had to arrange such meetings myself if I wanted to proceed with any degree of caution. At last I made it look as if my stronger nature were gaining victory over my principles, and I had to give only the slightest sign to see my lover in my own house and at my feet. And even then I capitulated, albeit with considerable composure, yielding at last with such phrases as to compel Herr von P—— to believe he was the first to triumph over me.

This Herr von P——, who, for all his vanity, was a creature of utmost good-heartedness, I succeeded in weaving into my interests in such a way that my involvement with him was not in the least disadvantageous. He confessed to me himself that his first efforts to win my favor had begun as the result of a wager; but he promised me at the same time that he was gladly willing to lose this wager once he had become convinced that I deserved respect. In trust he then gave me his hand, which I kissed. And he kept his word, like a good man; for as I know for certain, he not only paid off the wager as lost but also spoke of me in such phrases that my reputation could not but gain significantly.

Possessing a lover afforded me, I cannot deny it, inexpressible pleasure. To bind him still closer to me, I repeated with him what I had learned in Vaudreuil's school, yet did so in such a way that it appeared completely as if love had made me the inventor of all the arts I practiced upon him. But no matter how much pleasure all this afforded him, it still would not have held him had I not come upon a still better means of doing so. P——, though lacking any scholarly education, had a very highly developed understanding of social life; and since just the opposite was the case with me, I needed only to make myself his pupil to inspire in him attitudes towards me that he had never nurtured for a female being. For a loving woman, resignation costs nothing; and my strategy worked so well that P——, who, like many of his class, did not himself know the extent of his excellent inner qualities, felt in no small way flattered to be discovering within himself things he had never reckoned on finding. It is an eternal truth that love only diminishes with time and, when it can descend no further, will vanish into thin air like a chimera. It would have been impossible for me to hold fast to the fickle P—— for longer than a month had I not placed him above me as my teacher, had I not responded to his tutelage with eager comprehension, had I not made him the arbiter of my social behavior. I have known women who wanted to make themselves their lovers' tutors. They were fools who understood as little about love as I do about Hebrew. A man is simply not made to be taught by a woman, and in general I believe a woman must avoid nothing more than the appearance of deserving credit for a man's achievements. Henrietta of England, a princess of the House of Bourbon, sacrificed a dukedom for the charming Count de Lauzun, ceding it to King Louis the Fourteenth in order to free that adored count from the Bastille.[13] And what was her reward? She had to take that ungrateful man's boots off when he came home from the hunt and endure beatings from him as well. Gratitude is an all too demeaning feeling to coexist with a desire for freedom.

---

[13] Henrietta of England (1644–70) was the daughter of King Charles I of England and sister of Charles II. Sent to the court of King Louis XIV, she was ultimately unhappily married to the duc d'Orleans, the king's brother, and briefly flirted dangerously with the king himself. Duc de Lauzun was a favorite of the king but dispatched to the Bastille for insolent behavior in a jealous competition for another lady's favors. The predicament of Anonin-Nompar de Caumont, duke of Lauzun (1633–1723), described here in fact involved not Henrietta of England but Anne Marie Louise, duchess of Montpensier (1627–93), the daughter of Henry IV. On this factual error one of Wieland's male figures in the narrative "Rechtfertigung der berühmten Frau von Maintenon" bases his claim that the author of the *Confessions* must be a woman.

During my time with Herr von P——, I carried on all my old acquaintances. My behavior became ever more pleasing the more I observed. I spoke little, for I spoke with caution and always with deference to the judgment of others. The appearance of innocence could be no better preserved than by continuing to pay tribute to age. And this I did with a resignation that made no exceptions. If anyone courted my favor, I would be careful to distinguish between those whom I could assume were prepared for a lasting relationship and those whose social standing or other relationships allowed no such assumption. Those in the former group I would give all possible encouragement that could fire their interest; to those of the latter group I would, in a nice way, show my teeth, since I had no need of them. Nothing can ruin a woman's reputation more easily than when she enters into several love affairs at the same time, and the fact that my affairs have done me so little harm I owe especially to the loyalty with which I held to my lovers until such time as I found them to be either disloyal or burdensome.

P—— often told me he would marry me if he could have been even slightly convinced that he had not been spoiled for a relationship like marriage. I believe he was telling the truth on this point, too. Elsewhere I shall relate to you my beliefs on marriage, at which time it will be clear that I too should have had a thousand reservations about entering into such a relationship. As far as P—— is concerned, it never occurred to me to want to have him as a husband. I understood that at some time there would be a moment when our relationship would end; yet as long as this moment had not arrived, nothing, I was earnestly resolved, should hinder my full enjoyment of our love. To a few proposals of marriage made to me at just this time I gave not a single serious thought, even though they were worthy of consideration. People saw that as pride on my part, but it is often the case that other people find far better reasons for our actions than the ones actually guiding us. I considered it my good fortune to make these sacrifices for my P——, although I did not talk about them at the time at all, in part in order to avoid the appearance of obligation that would have turned him against me, in part out of the particular fear that he might have disapproved of what I was doing; for I knew him as an all too insightful man to be able to believe he could condone my frivolousness.

My affair with P—— had gone on for well over a year when it was sundered by a journey he was ordered from on high to undertake. Before his departure he told me that he considered our relationship to be completely over. I was hurt by this, since I had become accustomed to him; yet I became calm again as soon as I knew he was gone and began then to think of ways to make up for the loss I suffered with his sudden departure. My composure was the consequence of my loss. I shall never but take pleasure in thinking back on this affair; for it was not only the most enjoyable but also the most honest in which I was ever involved. Of all men, P—— best embodied the idea of a complete man that I had formed at an early age, a notion that I still held then and in which I was confirmed by nothing more than my involvement with him.

Put yourself, if you would be so kind, in my position. I had reached the age of seventeen, and I was on my own. My father cared as much about me as if I did not even exist or as if he were not my father—this without doubt as a result of the strange relationship in which I had lived with him. Gone was the support that P—— had been for me. Facing the world in that way, I felt like a person borne alone on the waves of an immense ocean. Since all my family ties had only a political purpose, none of them spoke to my heart; and since for the present even the political purpose had fallen away, I began to find these ties to be boring and disgusting. If at just this time I had found a decent match, I would have accepted it without reservation; and had my husband been even merely tolerable, despite all that had gone before, I would have become a tolerable housewife—not good and proper like you but still respectable enough at least not to make me look bad compared to the vast majority. But right at this time I could not find a good match, and so it was my fate to be carried away to new transgressions.

One of the homes I visited most frequently was that of Privy Councillor K——. Life in that household was unhappy, as was the case with most finer families; but the task was to keep that fact hidden from the world, while a significant fortune was sure to provide sufficient resources for that purpose. Nothing had made Madam Privy Councillor more desirous of my company than an assumed similarity between my mind and hers. She was infected by an enthusiasm for aesthetic pursuits and combined those interests with a high degree of false piety. Gellert was her hero, and she was never without one of his works in her hand.[14] Now, of course, I had recovered not only from my tendency to false piety but also from any form of piety at all; yet since I had retained my social adroitness and since the company I encountered in the K—— home could not be counted among the most uninteresting, I had no trouble positioning myself with my new friend in a way that convinced her she had found the right person in me. The privy councillor was the complete opposite of his wife. Despising aesthetic pursuits with all his heart and a confirmed freethinker, he

---

[14] Christian Fürchtegott Gellert (1715–69) played a decisive role in German literature's turn to the novel, especially in carrying on the English tradition of Samuel Richardson's epistolary novels with his *Das Leben der schwedischen Gräfin von G*** (1747–48; "The Life of the Swedish Countess von G**"). He was also an exponent of the fable and of religious lyric—for example, his *Geistliche Lieder* (1757; "Hymns").

lived only for his business and his pleasure. Nature itself seemed to have decreed him to be an Epicurean, and I do not recall ever seeing a man who could have struck me as better capturing the image of that Greek philosopher.[15] The men whom people commonly call Epicureans are obviously more closely related to swine than to humans; but K—— was different from these men partly by way of his lively and penetrating intellect, partly by the fact that work was really a need for him. Imagine now, on the one hand, a woman in poor health both physically and spiritually and, on the other hand, a man healthy in both respects, and you will be able to comprehend that there could be no hope of harmony between the two. Their relationship became still worse when K——, unable to leave off ridiculing his wife's weakness, also took it upon himself, as a loving father, to correct the twisted education his children were receiving.

I do not know how it came about that K—— noticed how I differed from his wife; but scarcely had he sensed that difference than he began to accord me special attention. For until then he had felt not only indifference towards me but also even animosity, on the assumption I was one of the pious sisterhood. Nothing fosters our

[15] Epicurus (c. 340–270 BC) was the founder of the Epicurean school, advocating reliance on the senses and propounding pleasure—that is, freedom from pain—as the highest good, gained through virtue and simple living. The association here of Epicureanism with sensual pleasure is a modern misunderstanding.

feeling of goodwill towards someone more than realizing that in our thoughts we have done them an injustice—just as, on the other hand, nothing intensifies animosity more than the actual commission of an undeserved insult. K——'s entire bearing seemed to say he was asking my forgiveness. I cannot tell you how interesting that made him for me. Yet since my relationship to P—— was still going on, I was most careful in hiding my feelings, and for some time I did not allow myself to dream that K—— could become dear to me.

As long as seduction is not a mutual impulse, it does not occur. The way people usually use that word makes no sense, whatever those who are weak of mind may say when they attempt to blame on others a wrong for which they alone are responsible. As long as I was still involved with my dear P——, K—— could have moved heaven and earth in an effort to win from me the slightest sign of favor, yet he would have struggled in vain. But now the situation had changed. The emptiness I felt in my life spoke in his favor, and so naught but the slightest wooing and courting was required for him to make, in short order, significant progress in gaining my favor. Moral feelings had given rise to his attraction to me. Similar feelings drew me to him. In this situation we could not fail to meet halfway. How often have I told myself that people would be less inclined to damn certain love affairs if they better knew what gave rise to them.

Keeping our relationship hidden from Madam Privy Councillor required no more than an ongoing pretense on my part and a little compliance from her husband. She, who would have been enraged if she had thought I was deceiving her, loved me like a sister when she saw that from time to time I would take the liberty to give her husband a good scolding when he was not nice to her, and that he in turn would meekly accept my rebuke and correct the error of his ways within a quarter hour. My position between the two resembled that of Madame de Maintenon between Louis the Fourteenth and his wife—albeit, of course, with a difference born of de Maintenon's greater genius in such matters—for such was her cunning that the queen would give daily thanks to God for turning her husband's heart towards her again through the powers of an angel in visible form, while at the same time that very angel . . . was denying herself nothing.[16] So great grew the trust my friend placed in me that I could dare to do things right before her eyes that people would never trust themselves even to think in the presence of a jealous wife. Since by and by I came to have the entire household totally in my hands, I did as I liked. It suited my interests that all relationships promising any kind of

[16] The narrator refers here to the marquise de Maintenon, Francoise d'Aubigné (1635–1719), who, as the widow of the crippled poet Scarron, became the governess of the children of King Louis XIV and his wife, Mme de Montespan. She later became the king's mistress (1674) and then his wife (1684).

disturbance should cease, and so cease they did. Most of the trysts with the privy councillor I had in my own quarters, which, as they had been transformed through P——'s generosity and my good taste into a veritable temple of Aphrodite, enhanced every pleasure. Since K—— had little understanding of his own love and since I took great care not to confide in him what I could call my secret, I had no difficulty in making him too believe he was the first to triumph over my modesty. That there were no explanations regarding such matters is self-evident. I would have lost everything if I had not been clever enough to avoid anything of that sort.

Of all the men with whom I had become involved at that time, K—— was the first whom I had totally in my power. The reason for that lay less in me than in his way of feeling and in his domestic situation. It was solely up to me if I wanted to move him to marry. What am I saying, "move him"? He proposed to me himself, claiming he would divorce his wife. I was uncertain for a moment, but only for a moment. In the first place, I could not imagine that a marriage founded upon deceit would be a happy marriage. In the second place, I feared the talk of my acquaintances, who it could be predicted would take sides with the spurned woman at my expense and decry me as the prime hypocrite. Without making mention of any of these reasons, I promised my lover I would become his wife when fate itself sundered the bonds that now tied him to a woman whom I could not make my enemy without causing her death. K—— was all too humane a man not to be deeply touched by such an answer.

But no matter how much I had enchanted the privy councillor, my relationship to him was still anything but suited to my inclinations. I have often thought—and it must surely be so, since so many events in life speak for it—that where fear is not in play, there can be no feminine love. The more rapidly K——'s personality was consumed by mine, the more quickly I was restored to myself. Habit surely played its role in this too, for since men had always dominated me before, it seemed to me as if it had to be so. In short: I became bored with K—— because he did not offer enough resistance. I tried to make him understand this in a great variety of ways; but it was my misfortune that on precisely this point he lost all sensitivity and clung to me with as much persistence as I exerted in trying to rid myself of him.

I found myself in no small dilemma, yet I was firmly resolved to break free of the bonds in which I had so frivolously ensnared myself. To approach my goal, I arranged for the trysts in my quarters to become ever more infrequent. I renewed contacts again that I had long ago given up. The time this all left me I devoted to Madam Privy Councillor. K——, who did not know what he was to think of me, pursued my every step. His passion seemed to have reached a peak it had never known before. Precisely this is what I wanted to happen, and since everything was now going according to my wishes, the catastrophe was totally in my power.

Towards Madam Privy Councillor I began to play the dejected one. Since she was not accustomed to seeing me that way, she inquired with all the more anxiety about the cause of my sadness. I spoke of our need to part company, but since she did not understand what I meant by that, she kept on at me until I explained: I had reason to believe her husband was beginning to nurture a secret affection for me. In this way I cast the first spark of jealousy into her soul; and since I saw very clearly how it caught fire, I merely asked that she trust my honesty.

A few days later I was, as usual, alone with the two of them. The madam arose and left, I knew not why. Scarcely had she left the room when K—— insisted on an explanation for my enigmatic behavior. I replied quite dryly that my behavior only seemed enigmatic, but that in essence it was open and honorable.

"So you no longer love me?" that emotional man asked, his tone whining as he cast himself at my feet. Without answering his question and without drawing attention to his position, I pressed a note into his hand and awaited the return of his wife, in order to set myself free with a kind of death-defying leap. She opened the door, was startled by the sight of her husband kneeling before me, and was about to turn around—when I suddenly arose, hurried to her, embraced her, asked her husband for forgiveness, and then bade her farewell forever. What the two did then, I do not know; but my note said that I considered it to be sinful to continue deceiving his wife any longer.

You will have to admit I must have understood something about the art of living, since I was capable of acting in such a manner. The misfortune most people complain about is merely the result of their indecisiveness; they cannot suffer each other, and still they cannot part from each other; they want to, yet they do not want to. And so their life runs on without joy or pleasure. To be one of them may bring honor to one's heart, but it never speaks well of one's reason. People who do not live in contradiction with themselves always find freedom, one way or another.

I resolved not to become involved in any new love affair, since the last had been made so unpleasant for me; but even without this resolve I would not have become so involved, since my father, soon after my break with the K—— household, became gravely ill. You will probably imagine that he would have kept me away from his deathbed in order to pay nature its last tribute in greater composure. He did no such thing! Of course I cannot say my presence gave him pleasure, but no more did it disturb him. His illness became prolonged, but he remained constant in his resignation from start to finish. I am sure none of the wise men of antiquity died with greater composure than he did. He was not so inwardly turned that he did not speak on occasion, and speak a great deal. Above all he put me in the picture about his fortune, and I can tell you that he knew right to the last penny how much he possessed. Then he spoke of my relatives and of what chance I would have with my brother and sister to improve our situation. Two hours before his death he said, "Soon it will be all over for me."

"All over?" I answered. "You do not believe in the immortality of your soul?"

He smiled. "My soul," he answered, "is immortal as all things are, it lives on in you."

These words struck me so, I have never been able to forget them. I closed his eyes. Old R—— helped me see to the burial. It cost me, as you can well imagine, a great struggle to bring forth the amount of tears propriety demanded; through all this, old R—— was as uplifted by my sensitivity as much as he had been by the good judgment I showed during the arrangement of the funeral, and the praise he accorded me on both points gave me to understand that I had played my role tolerably well.

I have completely lost sight of my brother and sister. My brother was at first to receive an academic education; yet since he had too little talent for that, he was consigned to the military. Since my mother's death I had not seen him again, for right after that he was sent to a good provincial school and from there to a distant garrison. My younger sister was taken into the household of one of my aunts who lived not too far from the capital. Raised in the countryside, she blossomed all the more beautifully the less hurried her upbringing was. She was, at the age of fourteen to fifteen years, innocence itself. Since we were so essentially different from each other, we were little suited to each other's company, although we did see each other from time to time. Having pretensions about me did not occur to her at all, but just for that reason she could not live up to any pretensions I had about her. We did not exactly quarrel, for we were too unlike each other for that as well; but we really could not bear one another. My propriety and my tone earned the approval of my aunt, and since the major portion of people do not know what qualities can go together in one person, that good woman would often point to me as an example for my naive sister, an ill-considered move that helped in no small way to turn Nettie—for that was my sister's name—even more against me. The result of it all was that after the death of my father I could find no welcome in my aunt's household and was thus left to continue on my own, to all appearances without shelter or refuge.

I had barely reached the age of eighteen; yet if you care to recall the events I have related to you up to this point, you must admit there are people of thirty or forty years of age who are less mature than I was in such tender years. Fate seems to have exerted all its powers to realize in my individual personality something that usually requires several generations to develop. I am not complaining; but why did I have to be the one on whom fate saw fit to do its experiments? Always it guided me upon other paths than I would have chosen to follow. Never was it my plan to be bad, and yet I have become so in an unavoidable manner. Perhaps you have already felt pity for me up until now, but you will pity me much more if you read on. The same love of truth with which I have revealed myself to you thus far shall continue to guide my pen. I have never read confessions that satisfied me, but for that reason I shall avoid the mistakes others have made. I will embellish or excuse nothing, and far less still will I justify anything. I will speak of myself as my good spirit would represent me if it were given the task of doing so.

Second Book

I would have continued my previous lifestyle had it been to my advantage. Appointed by my father to be my guardian, old R—— took an ever more lively interest in me; and since in the art of treating people according to their individual nature I had a better understanding than people expected from a person my age, and since my fortune was considerable enough to protect me completely from any form of servitude, I was very happy to accept the rules that my guardian was able to put in place to ensure me the protection I needed in order to be able to live free of any suspicion. He intended at the outset to take me into his home; but since that involved many difficulties, it was decided I was to be placed under the guardianship of one of my lady friends who had the best reputation in the world and who, with her large fortune, had acquired a considerable circle of followers.

You yourself are acquainted with Mamselle ——d, albeit not so closely that you would be able to give an account of her true character. There are certain books that, without actually being bad, have a very low worth simply because they do not stand up to a comparison with the originals they have to thank for their creation. An example of this sort of book is *The Christian Emile* by Formey, a book that most likely would never have been written had not Rousseau's *Émile* been such a sensation.[17] As with these books, so it is too with certain people; they would be accorded the respect they deserved if they could be spared certain comparisons in which they would necessarily come off the losers. Mamselle ——d can be characterized in a word by calling her "the Christian Ninon,"

[17] Johann Heinrich Samuel Formey (1711–97) was born of French parents in Berlin and educated there in theology and philosophy, eventually becoming a professor in philosophy. The year 1750 saw the completion of his novel-like work *La belle Wolfienne* with its advocacy of Christian Wolff's philosophy. In 1764 he wrote *L'Émile chretien*, an answer to Rousseau's *Émile, ou de l'éducation* (1762).

for like that lady she could never decide to give her hand to any man, but she did so not in order to remain free but rather to escape the oppressive feeling that she was sought after not for herself but for her money. Ninon, we know, had control over a great fortune; Mamselle has always been controlled by hers. In all truth we can say that her thoughts of her fortune were present at all times and in all situations, forming the basis of all her coquetries. As long as she was still young and men still had the hope of melting her resolve, she often looked as if she could well decide to marry; but basically she did that only so she could deliver a rejection in finest form and save for her old age the bleak consolation of having had no lack of suitors. In her later years she gained recognition by fostering the prospect that she might leave a legacy, yet without committing herself to any specific promise. She was never niggardly with her fortune. Never did she make any use of it of which people would not approve; but never did she gain from those many good deeds bestowed with generous hand any pleasure that was not rooted in her vanity; and by confining herself to this one meager feeling she spoiled a life that she could have made very pleasant with a greater commitment of heart and mind. I often observed in her presence that the wealthy who feel compelled to good deeds act counter to their best interests when they divide and disperse their gifts in order to enhance their body of followers and hangers-on.

They do not know the person; they seek to bind that person to them by making them dependent, even though they can really attain their goal only when they make that person free. Mamselle ——d erred completely by setting out to attract mainly clergymen, a class of people who, with few exceptions, cannot easily avoid going wrong, since their interests are so divided. Even at a young age I had earned the approval of Mamselle ——d. Now, when it was necessary to protect an orphaned child, she offered to take on the task. I had scarcely moved into her household than she began to indoctrinate me into all her maxims. It was her wish that I follow in her footsteps to become, like her, one of the vestal virgins. Nothing was dearer to her heart than to make me hate the entire male sex. What she called her experiences was an aggregation of acts of ingratitude and disloyalty by men against women. I listened to it all calmly and approved of her behavior, taking care only to make clear that each of us must measure events by our own standards and that what she might hold to be great insight could for others turn out to be the greatest folly should they lack the strength to make their own decision prevail.

I had lived in all too particular relationships with men of different types not to know what to think of marriage, and even the example of Mamselle ——d supported the truth of my conclusions. Without any specific principle or goal she let herself be borne on the sea of life, landing on any shore, seeking pleasure anywhere but finding boredom everywhere. She herself said repeatedly and constantly that one had to take life as a game; but only too deeply did she feel that life must have a serious goal if it is to remain at all bearable. Whatever one might say against marriage, its advantage quite rightly resides in the fact that it ennobles the female portion of the human race. Where there is no marriage, women are either children or monsters. Philosophers have dreamed of a community of women. Surely they thought that by doing so they were making a moral force out of the female sex; but this community, if it could ever be made possible, would have exactly the opposite effect. The basic goal can be only one and indivisible. If it becomes diverse, then it disappears, and that is all the more regrettable since the woman cannot do without such a basic goal. The exception of a Ninon does not count because such women are always the products of special circumstances. If life depends on living happily in a marriage, the requisites for success are, while not easy, still at least not impossible to fulfill. In society's higher circles, where women have more leisure time and, for precisely that reason, are most plagued by boredom, the problem is doubtless hard to solve; but in the middle classes a large portion of the difficulties disappears. Very much depends on whether the woman possesses the ability to develop her circle of influence so that it has no points in common with that of her husband. While all civic virtues must reside in him, all domestic virtues must reside in her. The business of earning and acquiring must be exclusively his, that of preserving and nurturing exclusively hers. The sciences, the arts, and so on exist for her only in reflected form; of all those pursuits she absorbs only the results, not caring how they came about. Unblemished by the filth of life, she is free of all the passions it brings. It may be in doubt whether virtue resides in her; but it is clear that she is burdened by no evil. Active without ostentation, well-meaning without affectation, she turns away all storms that could threaten her sacred realm. She possesses all those qualities her husband lacks, and since he has all those she cannot possess, the two form a whole that utters no false note and acts with a natural harmony. And as I thought and felt in this manner about marriage and the happiness it can give, I was far from concealing from myself the fact that if a certain innocence is a necessary ingredient for such a relationship, I could lay no great claims to attaining happiness therein; yet whether or not I was deluding myself on the point, I did not want to concede completely the necessity of this fact, and it seemed to me as if the degree of development I had acquired in place of innocence also had its worth. In short, Mamselle ——d so little succeeded in proselytizing me that she strengthened me instead in my resolve. Without taking issue with her in the least, I quietly held to my own side, firmly resolved henceforth not to ignore any advantageous opportunity that might present itself to me in the way of marriage.

As I accompanied Mamselle ——d everywhere, I very frequently came into the company of four spinsters of whom people said that as sisters they never wanted to separate. The Mamselles ——st possessed what, in their day, was no small degree of education. Striking at first glance was the extent to which they had all renounced any passionate feelings towards each other; among them there was no trace of jealousy, envy, and the like; each had her peculiarities, but was supported in them by the others. They would have gained a good deal of respect if it had been within their power to avoid one absurdity that made them the laughingstock of the whole capital. All aged spinsters and childless women share a tendency to strive to exhibit their worth as good citizens, whereby it appears that this is nature's way of punishing them for neglecting or not fulfilling their true calling in life. The Mamselles ——st outdid others of their sex by operating from their home an employment office, an operation that I would gladly call otherwise if I knew a better name for it. The business itself was the most innocent in the world and conducted as well with such unparalleled unselfishness that any would-be critic would have to blush to speak out against it. Ever striking was the way the four spinsters occupied themselves with finding support for artists, good positions for academics, and employment for male and female serving people. This kept them so busy that even the most assiduous planning left them little time to think of themselves. How many notes had to be written each day, some to make inquiries, others to make announcements! How much work went into keeping the register and conducting the correspondence! How besieged they were by unending requests and entreaties! Yet this all elicited from them not the slightest complaint, and no civil servant can be more devoted to his professional duties with greater selflessness than these ladies showed whenever they were called upon to be of aid to others with their contacts and credit.

The eldest of the four sisters—on whose behalf I must testify that her way of thinking gave evidence of much genuine philosophy—had no sooner noticed that my patroness was seeking to win me over with her man-hating maxims than she set to work to draw me to the opposing side, an enterprise that presented her with no great task, as my own inclinations were too much in her service.

"Our dear ——d," she would say, "is wrong. To become like her, one must feel an inner calling that no amount of preaching can instill. I would keep silent about it if you had sufficient means to assert your independence. What you have is just enough to help make life more pleasant; and precisely for that reason you must offer it to a man you love. You are supposed to marry, and you must. I insist you be happy, and I take upon myself the task of finding you a good husband."

I blushed at these words with so much modesty and propriety and thanked my Juno Pronuba so profusely for her generous concern for my fate that she could not but take a still more lively interest in me.[18]

As long as my father was still alive, men sought my hand with more caution than ardor, because they did not know what to think of his financial situation. Now things were reversed, because I let it be known, down to the last penny, what I possessed. Among these suitors there was a group of widowers, each asserting himself as well as he could. Yet as clearly aware as I was of the situation in which I lived, I could not accept the thought of becoming the wife of a widower, and that not out of the selfishness of which people so often accuse my sex but because I was loath to take the trouble of breaking old habits in order to acquire new ones in their stead. So all widowers, without exception, I rejected. Among the so-called young gentlemen, I made those distinctions that experience had taught me. My irrevocable principle was not to marry a merchant, because I could not imagine that any true marriage with one would be possible. Since my social standing left me only the choice between a military man and a so-called businessman, I directed my attention primarily

[18] In Roman mythology, Juno was the wife and sister of Jupiter and, in most of her forms, involved with marriage and childbirth. As Juno Lucina, she aided women in childbirth; as Juno Pronuba, she presided over betrothals and marriage.

to the latter class of men, simply because military men are suspected, where their relationships to the bourgeois are concerned, of paying too close attention to money.

Many approached me, but none among them pleased me as much as did Military Councillor V——. So ineffably great were the goodwill and kindness of his expression, and so paired they were with evidence of healthy, sound reason, that few men could compete with him. True, he had not the colossal figure with which Vaudreuil and P—— had charmed me so; but since he was not a small man and gave evidence of a sound constitution, I soon discarded this one requisite, which I myself must admit was born more of fantasy than of reason. Thus to him did I accord the most cordial reception; and since the ——st sisters did not refrain from lauding in him every possible good quality—to the extent that even my patroness was compelled to join in praising him—I soon ended the usual period of deliberation by accepting his proposal without restrictions or reservations.

You will not be surprised when I tell you that my comportment as a bride was deemed quite proper by all those who are past the time in life in which they become enthused about something, but that on the other hand it was deemed remarkable by all those who are of the opinion that a woman should lose her senses at the good fortune of finding a husband. Those of the latter type asked me constantly whether I did not love my husband—a question that I found less embarrassing than people might have thought, since I was aware of my superiority to all my young female friends. I answered them by saying that marriage was for me a much more serious matter than it was for them, since I was now alone in the world and as a result had much more to risk. "But he's such a good man," my friends said. "That I have yet to see," I responded.

No time passes more quickly than that of newlyweds. In a twinkling I had become Madam Military Councillor. My patroness, as confirmed a spinster as she was, did not fail to wish me happiness from the bottom of her heart and, by way of atoning for the sarcastic remarks she had made about marriage, said that she had not believed the male sex could have harbored the likes of V——. My Juno Pronuba was heartily pleased that I was acting so sensibly, and she prophesied the happiest of marriages for me, and I myself could not imagine an unhappy one.

How fundamentally confessions differ from a novel! My story would be over now if it were the product of fantasy. But since it is something real, it is basically now just beginning. What had happened to me before can be excused in many ways—by my youth, by the strange upbringing and education accorded me, by the unusual situations in which I lived—the important thing is merely to have the good intentions of looking for reasons, and they are sure to be found. What is now about to begin—must

I pronounce myself guilty? For now I shall say to you only that I shudder merely to survey the events and that I do not know where I am to find the courage to continue with my confessions.

You might imagine that with the fickleness typical of my sex I gave up my ideal of a happy marriage even in the first days of my union with V—— and, having encountered a more charming man, audaciously forsook my word and duty to give preference to him. You would be wrong. Never has an abstract ideal been more completely realized, and never has anyone known a better marriage than I. V——, who loved his work as a businessman, pursued it with the zeal of an exemplary citizen. I lived and thrived in my domestic sphere. We both loved pleasure, but we were both incapable of enjoying it without the other. Our financial earnings were not dazzling but sufficient. We had no so-called bosom friends, but we were all the better for it, for there was no one to betray us. Those with whom we associated touched us no more and no less than is necessary to feel oneself free of egotism of the more offensive variety, while at the same time retaining a clear and independent mind. At times I would quietly reproach myself with the conviction that my situation would have been better if I had remained more innocent. But I quickly retreated from such notions in order not to become preoccupied with them. V—— seemed incapable of any strong passion; in me, all passions seemed to have run their course and died out. One day went by like the other, none of them totally bereft of pleasure. If I could not be in my husband's company, then I lived in the company of my lady friends, who did not cease to consider me happy. In this manner more than two years passed.

In the meantime my younger sister had married as well. Time, as well as ending the interest that once caused childish discord between us, had brought about another interest that, without being too lively, bound us together in sisterly fashion. To maintain this interest, the distance between us at this time may have been very necessary, yet this was something that neither of us thought about. Quite unexpectedly my sister informed me that she had been happily delivered of a baby boy. This news, which should have pleased me, left me feeling more lonely than I had ever felt before. I thought of my own childlessness. Before I was married, I had never thought of wanting children; I tended rather more to abhor a thought that ran so counter to my own happiness. Since my marriage to V—— I had occasionally felt the desire to have children, but never very strongly and, as I thought, rather more out of devotion to my husband, who, like all gentle and virtuous men, had mentioned more than once that he would like to father a child. But barely had I finished my sister's letter than I sank into a sadness that from that moment on I could not control. My jealousy of my sister strengthened my love for my husband.

"Why," I asked myself, "must the modest wish of the best of men remain unfulfilled? Why?"

To this question there were many answers. One lay in my previous life, especially in my relationship with Vaudreuil. I thought back on him with loathing. But was he to bear the guilt for my barrenness so completely alone? What part of my inner constitution had he destroyed? Wasn't I completely healthy? Did I not then have to seek the cause of my unfruitfulness in myself? The more I became caught up in these doubts and uncertainties, the more confused I became. One flood of tears would follow the next. Never has a transformation occurred more suddenly.

V—— did not know what to think of all this and kept at me until I told him the cause of my distress. To calm me, he said that the desire for children was one of those wishes that a happy husband cannot easily part with; but he would renounce it with all his heart if it threatened to disturb our harmony. As well, he went on, I was wrong to give in to the thought that I was damned to remain barren; my youthfulness and my health bode well for the possibility of having children; as with any other happiness, we would simply have to wait calmly for this one. I embraced him for this magnanimous comment, while resolving to follow his advice, but my reassurance was short-lived.

I maintain that a barren woman must never think of her destiny if she is not to lose the guiding tramontane of her life's ensuing voyage; at least my own experiences force me to say this. There are feelings that language cannot express because men have given them form and women have received them. One of these feelings is the desire to become a mother, although one cannot exactly insist that it ranks foremost among powerful drives. Few women have known this feeling, because nature has been kind enough to anticipate their desires, and to all these women what I have just said will seem silly exaggeration—this unless those who find themselves in my situation can bear witness that I am writing the truth; only to them can I appeal; they alone can judge me.

So do not be surprised when I tell you that the thought of my childlessness never left me and became a veritable torment for me. This went so far that I began to loathe that there was only one way to have children. Dissolved in tears, I lay at my husband's side and cried out, "Why can I not have children?" And when, after I had made such an outcry, my husband would try to embrace me, I would pull away from him and exclaim, sobbing, "But I still shall not have children!" Here I am lifting the veil that conceals the unhappiness of many a marriage; but why should I not do so, since this side of female nature most often goes unrecognized and misunderstood by men? My strange behavior—which would well deserve to be faulted as unreasonable if human beings had command of reason—had a devastating effect on my husband.

What by nature's plan is supposed to be an act of voluptuous enjoyment cannot be brought about by pain and despondency; and the more intense the sympathy that V—— showed for my condition, the more his constitution lost its vitality without there being any outward sign of his weakness.

As our relationship was worsening in this way day by day with virtually no prospect of improvement, my husband came upon the idea of adopting the child of one of his distant relatives who was living in impoverished circumstances. To this idea I responded with a wholehearted "Yes!," promising myself from such an arrangement at least the illusion of change. At that time we were going through the era of pedagogy with its mania for hoping to improve the world through certain modifications of the educational system. People discussed the writings of Locke and Rousseau; people wrote books for children; they inveighed against certain secret evils; they recommended cold baths, and so on and so forth. Since I had no lack of free time, I shared the general mood among the intellectuals. Eagerly I read the writings of a Campe, a Trapp, a Villaume, a Bahrdt, a Stuve, and so on.[19] Of course I did not find the results I was hoping for; yet the

[19] Joachim Heinrich Campe (1746–1818), Ernst Christian Trapp (1745–1818), Peter Villaume (1746–1825), Carl Friedrich Bahrdt (1741–92), and Johann Stuve (1752–93) were all Enlightenment-age writers on didactics and education in the tradition of Locke, Rousseau, and Pestalozzi.

more I read and the more, as a result, my body of ideas grew, the more I tended to lose sight of the results. I was most attracted by Villaume's writings, which had best mastered the art of confusing with clarity and could thus most easily deceive. At present I think about all matters that pertain to the education system quite differently; but I confess that I was most enchanted by the subject and that my reading—or rather my painstaking study—of those writers intensified my desire for a child in no small measure.

Through adoption I had, as if by magic, what I had been longing for so intensely; and even though I told myself from the start that the child of a distant relative was not my child and never could be, I still thought it magnanimous to devote the greatest of care to the child's upbringing. I was firmly resolved to apply the full range of the arts of upbringing and education to the child entrusted to my care, and I dreamt of the brilliant success with which I would be rewarded. So Emilie—that was the name of our relative's daughter—was brought to our home. She was then about twelve years old. By all my expectations, she would be delighted by my motherly behavior towards her; yet this was not the case; she remained totally indifferent. Was it my fault or hers?—I do not know; but the blow that my self-esteem suffered from this incomprehensible coldness from the very outset gave my feelings a turn that was not very favorable to my purpose. The more the mother was driven out of me, the more the teacher in me took her place. As an artist I was much too inclined to see everything in the light of its faults. I did not cease to indoctrinate, and since my indoctrinating was without success, I soon became despotic. Now I had ruined everything; but that I myself was to blame for it, I could see all the less clearly, the more I remained conscious of my good intentions. Had Emilie been my own daughter, nature would have protected her from all tyranny; but since she was not, nothing was able to save her. I admit I treated her barbarically, yet I did it not to torment her but rather out of devotion to the principles that I had taken up from the writings on education and that I held to be unimpeachable. Philanthropy transformed in my hands into the most abominable rigor; but I am sure that under the conditions that were guiding me, this was a natural and inevitable result. The more intent I was on turning Emilie into an obedient tool, the more obstinate she became, and as that increased, so did my tyranny, not ending until Emilie took advantage of my absence and forced her way to freedom, running back to her father.

Since then I have never again made an attempt to raise a young person; but I have come to know human nature better. And noting human nature's inclination to contain little that is positive, as well as the fact that the human race is caught up in an ongoing process of development—

the participation in which must be the highest goal of the individual—I have come to see any notion of positive upbringing and education to be pure and inexcusable foolishness. Were it ever to occur, it could be brought about only if one were to have total control of all situations, which would require, in addition to an immense fortune, that one deprive the poor pupil of all freedom and turn him or her into a mere machine—and even the thought of such a procedure is enough to enrage a person. For though we are but tools of a nature that, all things considered, always achieves the opposite of what we would wish to happen, we nevertheless are still ultimately formed and shaped by human willfulness.

As unfortunate as my experiment with Emilie was, it had still been a diversion for me. But this positive effect ceased the moment she returned to her father and I had calmed down about the defamatory comments that her running away had caused—for it lay in the nature of the whole affair that I was decried as an evil woman, who, not satisfied with mistreating her husband, had also brought her satanic behavior to bear upon a defenseless young girl. My desire to have a child of my own became all the more intense, the more isolated my way of life became and the less inclination I felt to escape my loneliness. My husband, who just at this time was immersed in professional matters, did not have the time to worry about my situation; and then he had no sooner noticed what was happening within me than he offered up every bit of his friendliness in an effort to ease my pain and cheer me up. We had arrived at the silent agreement that we would speak no more of my barrenness; but exercising the greatest of delicacy is not always the best way to maintain a good relationship. I had to clear the air; and since I did not dare do so to V——, in order not to make him feel depressed, I poured out my secret to others.

I have always noticed that people find nothing so pleasant as the discovery of intense passions in someone else. Do they know by some kind of instinct that a person in such an impassioned state is at her weakest? At any rate we are never without the desire to dominate, and as a result of that desire we constantly feel constrained to exploit the weaknesses of others wherever we come upon them. No sooner had I confided in others about my inner state than a host of helpful spirits came forward claiming to be in possession of infallible means of ensuring fertility. To how many secret cures did I subject myself, and how dearly have I paid for doing so! The sole result of all the experimenting was that my health was still further undermined than it had been as a result of the grief gnawing at my heart. My husband, who had no inkling that I had resorted to quackery, had the most heartfelt sympathy with my condition; and since by all appearances I was on the verge of wasting away completely, he insisted that I entrust myself to the care of a discreet doctor. This I did.

The advice of the doctor was that I should visit a spa. I had anticipated this advice, and as much as I doubted that a spa would bring any improvement, I still did not want to deny myself the satisfaction of knowing that I had tried that cure as well.

A stay at a spa is made pleasant by the many diversions it entails. I believe that the baths can be an excellent way of alleviating certain illnesses. But in the battle against an organic defect they are just as ineffective as any other means. I found my stay in Pyrmont cheering,[20] but I became no more fertile. My stay there even affected me adversely as a result of what people are wont to call the liberties of spa life, but what should properly be termed moral license. Indeed, a person should reach a certain age in order to be able to visit the baths without encountering problems. Everything there favors mutual seduction; and even though I was not untrue to my husband, I still sensed in myself a laxity that I never noticed in myself before and that could have been nothing else but the product of bad examples I could not keep from noticing.

My good cheer deserted me again as soon as I found myself back within my own four walls. People depend so much upon their environment that they can deny their chameleon-like nature only by taking no notice of

[20] Bad Pyrmont, a locality in Lower Saxony known since the sixteenth century as a spa offering curative mineral waters, was visited in 1744 and 1746 by Frederick the Great, king of Prussia.

it. My state was worse than before, since I had become halfway accustomed to diversion. But pursuing only the one thought and so immersed in this thought that I could think of nothing else, I subjected myself to inconceivable torment. There were bright moments in which I called myself a fool; yet I gained nothing by doing so other than the disconsolate self-admission that I was not the master of my own passions. To cut off my every retreat into an excuse I told myself, "Your barrenness is Vaudreuil's work, and since in that case it is unavoidable, you must accept it." But that was merely a way to bring myself to despair. I was like a raving madwoman who does not herself know what she wants.

After this confession you will find it understandable and perhaps even forgivable when I tell you that after I had lost my faith in the effectiveness of my secret remedies, I gave myself over to superstition. I have often noticed that a person can be an atheist and still believe in miracles with the shortsightedness of an old wife if some form of passion is in play. This is exactly what I experienced, and to such a high degree that I would have embraced Gypsy women if I could have found any. When I heard of an old woman who was versed in so-called mental telepathy, I would seek her out and make her my confidante, asking her to support me with her art. I was ashamed of myself as I did so; but Hell itself could have opened up before me to frighten me back from taking such a course, and

I would sooner have plunged into the abyss than turn back. I had always heard that card readers were cheats and swindlers, and no one could have been more convinced of this than I was, but none of that deterred me from seeking with them a cure for my troubles. It is obvious that these doings and dealings cost me considerable sums of money; but does money have any value at all when a person is trying to satisfy a great desire? Would you say that I had completely lost my mind? I surely had, as long as I was giving my passions free rein; but I was anything but insane when necessity demanded that I control my passion. In company, people did not notice in the least that anything was wrong with me, even though I cannot deny that I was very quiet towards my friends and acquaintances. I was actually ashamed of myself, and my downcast gaze dates from this time. Before that I had not had the least trouble looking each and every person straight in the eye; but did I not have to become habitually shy the moment I saw myself among those whom I had once so proudly looked down upon?

I was determined to go to ever greater lengths. An old woman in whom I confided was a Catholic, and she said to me that her priest would be able to help me. I laughed; but because she was completely serious and cited several miraculous cures that he was supposed to have effected, I deigned to make her priest's acquaintance. It was left to me whether I wanted to meet this helpful adviser in my home or his, or at some third place. I found a third place most convenient. We agreed on a location and time, and I arrived as planned. The priest was already there. In his expression was the slack resignation announcing that his battle with the flesh was over but testifying at the same time to the fierceness with which that battle had been fought. I imagine that meeting face to face, we must have offered a very picturesque scene. The priest squinted at me, all cold seriousness, while I stood before him with downcast eyes, unable to find words. But he took the lead, saying that he had heard so many good things about me that he wanted to help me, even though I was not one of his flock. Then he asked many questions that, coming from his mouth, caused me to blush repeatedly and that I am forced to leave to you to guess. He then took a holy relic out of his pocket and asked me to sit down beside him.

I began to feel boiling hot; but I followed him to a settee. First he asked me to hold out my right hand. I did; and after he had looked at it for a long time, he gently moved the relic over my hand, touching it lightly and making three signs of the cross. I confess to you that I had a wondrous feeling while he was doing that. Perhaps my imagination was causing my strange feelings; but since they were quite new to me, I believed all the more in the effect of relics. He then insisted that I open my bodice. I wanted to stop; but when he made me take seriously to heart that someone desiring the end must also approve the means, I yielded to him on this point as well. He repeated his procedure on my left breast, and it had quite the same effect. Finally, he insisted that I offer the tip of my tongue. This I brought myself to do without hesitation, and saltpeter is no colder than what I imagined I was feeling. At that point he looked upon me with lust.

"You have received the means of grace," he said, "but now the means of nature must also come into play."

And with these words he embraced me and pressed his lips to my bosom. I endured what I had lost the strength to resist, and he exploited my condition so well as to triumph over me repeatedly. When at last he told me that we had done enough for one day, I parted from him in I know not what state of numbness, from which I did not recover until I had arrived back home.

The mood in which I found myself after I was thinking clearly again was a very peculiar one. I felt inclined to please my husband in every way, yet I told myself at the same time that I had ruined our relationship forever. It is a strange contradiction of human nature that we cannot insult another person without also hating that individual! I have felt this contradiction in all its intensity, but I have never been able to understand it properly. Do we strike a hateful pose in anticipation, in order to ward off the attack we fear? But if that is the case, why do even those people hate who have no attack to fear? Why do parents hate their children, and regents their subjects, after they have insulted them? Wherever the key to this secret of nature may lie, it is clear that only those who have been insulted are able to forgive from their hearts.

My husband was so surprised by the change I had undergone that he never tired of telling me how charming I was! This statement did not surprise me, because I knew that a ray of sunshine is all the more pleasing, the more seldom it occurs and the more dreary have been the days upon which it follows. But what did surprise me was the strange mix of well-meaning and hateful feelings I felt within myself for my husband, a mix that, first of all, merely suppressed the respect in which I had once held him and that then put me in a mischievous mood that was otherwise quite new to me. I had one foolish notion after the other. V—— laughed about it; I laughed with him. Had I always been so cheerful, he said, then I would not have remained barren. This surprising combination, born of innocence, cut me like a knife; but I composed myself and retained my petulant mood through the following days.

With the priest I had arranged to meet again in a week at the same place where we first came together. We were in the same room again. There was no more talk of the means of grace; these had done their work for good and all. On the other hand, the means of nature were employed anew, and the priest, who became increasingly free and self-assured, by and by laid aside all his seriousness and made himself as charming as a—priest can make himself. What would you expect? It lies in human nature that a person, in addition to the qualities that he really possesses, wishes for others that will remain ever foreign to him. The donkey in the fable, who, not happy with being merely a useful animal, also wishes to play the chamberlain, is all too common a figure. The priest I found to be a most ridiculous lover; but once I had elevated him to that status, I enjoyed myself with him as best I could.

I would lead you through a revolting sequence of love scenes if I went into detail about the encounters I had with the priest. The affair lasted longer than it should have. And need I tell you that it was totally unsuccessful in satisfying my wishes? Likely I do, since gentlemen of this type have a reputation for being the best helpers in times of need. And since I had the courage to act first in putting an end to the relationship, he had the audacity to tell me that the result would have been quite different if he had not been dealing with a heretic. Duplicity of this sort has become a habit to people of this type. Nothing can be said to refute that.

The filth that covers my confessions would arouse nothing but repugnance if I did not at the same time tell, along with my aberrations, of the transformations occurring within me. The human heart is an inexhaustible treasure trove of observations; and as I continue to present these with all the precision expected of me, I hope to triumph still further over the disgust I cannot help imparting to you along with the confessions themselves. So know then that in my relationship with my husband I began to feel all the lighter at heart, the more I trampled upon my duties. Domesticity totally lost its worth in my eyes. I craved pleasure more and more. I came to need drama and theater in particular, and I missed no concert, no public entertainment. My husband's world was turned upside down. The expenses we went to for all this exceeded our income by far. Such were the causes and the results of my charm.

Amid all this rash and downright lascivious behavior, I observed the caution of respecting my own sex. The better I knew its weaknesses, the more I held to my old tactic of avoiding them, since I was convinced I could save my reputation only in this way. The actress ——b—— was then the toast of the town. She became the center of a circle of those people who knew no other calling in life but to enjoy pleasure. There was talk of nocturnal orgies that she would arrange and host. I had known this woman for some time, and my own inclinations pointed quite clearly to a life of dissolution; nor was there any lack of invitations to take part in such a life. Yet my fear of adverse gossip gained the upper hand, and far from aligning myself with the lascivious ones among my sex, I moved only in those social circles whose company lifts even the most suspect woman above suspicion. Since every coterie of women has its leader figure, I would attach myself especially to her; and the tribute that I paid her vanity by submitting to her wishes at every opportunity inevitably succeeded in ensuring that public opinion was always on my side. Recalling that I really did not lack social talent, you will not doubt my veracity when I tell you I was welcome everywhere. The great intellectual deficiency of most women worked in my favor.

I had at this time the good fortune to please a man of high government rank who had often encountered me in society and been in no small measure enchanted by my gifts. His Excellency was the Minister Z——. Turning down a love affair was no longer a notion I entertained seriously, and although this minister bore little attraction for me, still simply the fact that a minister was courting my favor sufficed to banish any doubts on the matter. We are doubly inclined to take up with those who wield power or are at least believed to do so. The preliminaries were much more elaborate this time than they usually tend to be. Numerous intermediaries were marshaled at His Excellency's behest, yet I was so cunning as to reject all offers that came to me through third parties. I wanted to determine the conditions myself and in fact ultimately did ensure that they were set by me alone. Rooms were found and rented in an outlying district of the city, and there we held our trysts. No one there knew us, and the pleasures of our liaison could have been much enhanced by this seclusion had the minister's personality allowed it. People of his kind have, at a certain age, become so accustomed to presenting themselves in an official public role that they are inclined to do so even at a romantic rendezvous. To treat me as a priestess of the lowly Venus would not do; to please me by casting off his ministerial glory seemed impossible. So how were we two to get along? Semele was a fool for requesting of Jupiter the favor that he come to her arrayed in all his awful splendors.[21] Far from following the example of her fate, I set out quite assiduously to defeat my lover's hauteur; for quite aside from the fact that I found all this putting on of official airs distasteful, I also had to reap some compensation for the meager pleasures that this love affair otherwise provided. My mockery seemed to work at first, yet a man of no great imagination can be led to no great adventure. As the saying goes: Short hair is quickly shorn. The minister retreated much too quickly into his official role. Our trysts became ever more seldom, the more often he felt he was being insulted, and the end of the story was that

[21] Semele becomes the mother of Bacchus when Jupiter comes to her as a lover. She then agrees to participate in the test of Jupiter's identity by asking him to appear to her in all the splendors he wears in heaven. Bound to grant her request, Jupiter adorns himself in his heavenly splendors, but not in all his terrors. When, thus arrayed, he enters Semele's chambers, her mortal frame cannot endure the splendors of his immortal radiance, and she is reduced to ashes.

he took his revenge in a way that very much suited his character but was all the more hurtful for me.

He requested that I come to another tryst. I appeared as arranged. I encountered in his stead his valet. That fellow had the audacity to tell me that his master wished that I might carry on my affair with him. I stared at him, eyes wide; but without letting that hold him back, he took the liberty of trying to kiss my hand while declaring his love for me in finest form. This was a blatant insult. To ensure myself at least some small satisfaction, I gave the lout a sound slap, and before he regained his senses, I was already in my carriage.

I confess that I needed some time to overcome the disgrace of this incident; it hurt me so deeply that I would have gladly given up on love affairs. Yet it is not easy to turn back after one has covered a long distance, and the behavior of my husband contributed in no small way to keeping me on the path I had chosen. Convinced of my disloyalty without having proof of it in hand, he took a stance that allowed me the greatest freedom, namely he immersed himself in his work—in part to forget his domestic unhappiness, in part to give himself an excuse for treating me with such indifference. I did not remain unaware of these maneuvers, but I acted as if I did not notice. I went so far as intentionally letting him believe that it was my desire not to be a burden to him that was keeping me out of the house more. He said nothing about it, nor did he in even the remotest way remind me of past times. All too much kindness can be harmful. Had V—— exhibited some vigorous passion, had he called me a woman of loose morals and threatened to turn me out, I would not have endured such reproaches in cold blood, to make the truth of them at least a matter of doubt; but I would have begun to be fearful and in fear would have acted with wisdom. But the way V—— behaved now, I could dare what I wished, for all about his bearing showed that he had accepted his fate and that he was expecting the future to bring still worse. Indeed, the compliance of most husbands is the ruin of their wives, and husbands who have given up the hope of emerging victorious in the battle of strength against cunning are burying the hope of any domestic happiness. And thus did my husband's apathy let me be drawn anew into the maelstrom.

A raging passion by which I had been seized for one of the most popular actors I renounced at once, as I saw that I had too many rivals in that pursuit. For although it is not always impossible in such situations to emerge victorious, the victor always runs the risk of gaining her triumph at the price of her reputation.

It was in one of the most lovely springtimes that I made the acquaintance of the witty N——. While we soon arrived at a mutual understanding, we remained uncertain as to how we wished to enjoy each other's company. Love is a diamond that, once one has become accustomed to possessing it, can give pleasure only by new settings found for it. I had had enough of being passed from one hand to another without enjoying in the process some other form of variety beyond that provided by the change of partners. Not merely the actors but the theater as well I now wanted to change. To set this plan in motion, I sounded out my husband as to whether he might like to move to one of the villas surrounding the capital city. "Let us just live totally for ourselves," was how I phrased my invitation. V—— responded with the same calmness with which he reacted to everything I did and gave in on this point too. We soon found the villa that we wanted to move into. Upon my signal, N—— then found rented lodgings in the same neighborhood, and I had the pleasure, on the evening of the very day that we moved out of the capital, of hearing him play the flute for me.

My husband surely had no idea what to think of all this, but since he was always, at the first sign of changed attitudes, disposed to conciliation, he now believed more than ever that I was being honest with him. In addition, the sojourn in open nature served to suppress the professional man in him and bring joy to his human side. His face radiated an unaccustomed cheerfulness when, the next morning, the sunshine awakened him earlier than usual. He asked me to arise as well and accompany him on a walk. Off we went, and barely had we entered deep into the woods that adjoined our villa than he took my hand, addressed me by my first name, reminded me of the first years of our marriage, and implored me to grant him again the love for him that he had always deserved. He was putting me to a difficult test. I was sorely tempted to confess to him the wrong that until now he had only sensed. But, my composure soon regained, I embraced him. There was nothing I could do but place all blame on him. I did so gently, and, good-natured as he was, he admitted to having neglected me, as he had come to imagine he no longer meant anything to me. I knew I mustn't let the discussion draw out too much, since it would have required too many explanations. Accordingly, I broke it off as soon as was possible, and by playing the innocent to the utmost of my talent for illusion, I regained the full trust of my husband.

The entire scene quite properly made me reflect upon myself again, and I confess I had trouble mastering the compunctions that threatened to gain power over me. For when my husband, after a few hours, had left me to attend to his affairs in the city and I was left completely to my own reflections, I was so unable to withstand the surge of feelings that reproached me for my degradation that I broke into a flood of tears, loathing my life and wishing I were dead.

"For years now caught up in a steady decline," I said to myself, "how will you end? All you have saved is a reputation that is worthless if it is not based on a clear conscience. You betray your husband, who merits all your respect and has no fault other than being too good for you. And how do you betray him? What man have you ever rejected? Do you consider it to be to your merit that you have not given yourself to many more men? Have you not made immorality as much a habit as your husband has virtue? And what is the source of all this madness? Do you have the least right to make anyone else accountable for your barrenness but yourself? Is not your unthinking association with Vaudreuil the cause of everything—?"

I was in the midst of this monologue when I heard N——'s flute, reminding me of our affair with the little song from the *Magic Flute*—"A sweetheart or a little wife. . . ."[22] Never has a tragic mood been more comically interrupted. At first I was upset at the fatal coincidence in play; but when N—— did not tire of tootling his little song, I ultimately had to break out in loud laughter. If there are some people who need no pretext to be good, then there are also others whom no pretext helps to become good, and to this latter group I had every reason to count myself. Even after N—— had stopped playing, the tune kept echoing in my ears: "A sweetheart or a little wife," and so on. I sang the song as he had played it. All earnestness

[22] In aria 20 in act 2, scene 6, of Mozart's opera, Papageno sings "Ein Mädchen oder Weibchen / Wünscht Papageno sich! ("A sweetheart or a little wife / Is Papageno's wish!" [62, 63]).

was dispelled from my soul. Mechanically I began tidying things as if expecting a visit. I pondered how I would have to dress in order to show I lived in the country. I stood at the mirror surveying my charms. In short, I forgot all but the merest memory of what had happened in the hours before; and after I had put on a tasteful negligee, I went out into the garden to enjoy, as I told myself, the springtime air in full measure, but in fact to let N—— know that I had well understood his little song. I am still astonished when I think back on the sudden change that occurred in me in that brief span of time.

N—— no sooner saw me step out the back door than he came following me. The garden wall separating us was low enough that we could see each other, and the gardens were much too deep for any curious eyes to follow us. At the farthest end of my garden was an arbor of woodbine, and scarcely had I entered it than N—— leapt the wall and joined me there. He was curious why I had made him wait so long before giving any sign of life. I recalled the sign he had given me, and when I had to laugh about it again, he did not cease inquiring about the cause of my laughter, until I told him about the scene played out between my husband and me. I had not finished the story when he too, guessing the ending, broke out braying in laughter.

"Are you not on good terms with your husband, then?" he asked. I blushed.

"You're in the wrong there," he went on, "a woman must never spoil things between herself and her husband; better to give up a dozen lovers instead. I have courted many an honorable woman, but I have never insisted she should love me exclusively."

That was saying much; yet certain people have the privilege of being able to say anything and go unpunished for it, and N—— was one of these. Of all my lovers, he was the least inclined to take love seriously. Even at our first meeting he was so ardent that I had to yield to him. With that he suggested that we cross the small bridge that led to a small woods, grown dense with nothing but acacias and rowan trees. The pleasant aromas wafting our way brought with them the spirit of desire. We did not grow tired of our caresses. As full of pulsing life as the nature surrounding us, we did not return from the woods until the greater warmth of the midday sun told us it was time to end our mischievous play. On the way back I told my friend he would have to court the favor of my husband if we were to have unimpeded opportunity to see each other, and he promised me he would do his part.

If ever a person was adept at dealing with every relationship in life, it was N——. That very day he encountered my husband in the park, as if by chance, and drew him at once into a conversation that could not but win him over with its seriousness and sense. Without any originality, but giving the most consummate impression of it, he broke off as soon as he had made a lasting impression, taking his leave without having asked with whom he had been conversing. V——, upon returning home, could not keep from telling me about the intellectual eccentric whose acquaintance he had just chanced to make. From his description I knew at once that N—— had to be this eccentric, and I made fleeting reference to a desire to be part of the company. They encountered each other in the same manner in the following days, until both men made the discovery that they were neighbors and promised to visit each other. Soon after that, my husband requested that I invite Herr N—— to visit us at midday, and thus he appeared at the request of my husband himself. If N—— played his role well, I played mine no worse. Cool politeness can be taken no further than I took it. Curious, V—— asked me, after N—— had left, what I thought of him. Very well for a man of knowledge, was my answer, but very badly for a man of reason. V—— remarked with a smile that women could never forgive a man for possessing something that went beyond their kind of wit, and to this I remained silent, because I could not have heard anything more to my advantage.

As soon as my husband had developed a liking for N——, I continued my affair with N—— all the more undisturbed; and if my rural sojourn had promised a whole range of new pleasures, I was not deceived in my expectations. N—— was inexhaustible in inventing new scenarios; and as agilely as my imagination followed him, it was not a rare occurrence that he surprised me. The fact that every notion of propriety was alien to him goes without saying; how else could I have found him pleasing! If we were entertaining company and it suited him to take part, I would introduce him as a friend of my husband and whisper to my closer acquaintances that he was an intolerable philosopher who could offer amusement only when played for a fool.[23] These assurances N—— would do nothing to contradict, and as great a master as he was in the art of deception, the deception was made all the easier for him in this case by the fact that the people he encountered in our home were as aged as they were boring.

Our affair lasted through the summer, and it would have been difficult to find a cozy spot within a quarter league of our garden that was not witness to our love. Since N—— wished to leave the capital for the winter, he parted from me as jovially as he had entered my life, only that he mixed a bit of meanness into his parting, in order, as he told me later himself, to take revenge on me for imposing on him my constant deceptions.

It was one of the loveliest days early in the autumn when he asked me to go on our last walk together. We

[23] The German uses the verb *türlipinieren*, a variation of *turlupinieren*, which Grimms' dictionary defines as "to make unkind fun of someone" and traces back to the French *turlupiner*, based on the name Turlupin, a comic figure in seventeenth-century French drama.

passed once again through the whole area, in order, where possible, to recall every pleasure that had brought us such bliss through those four months. At last he came to a stop at one of our favorite spots. "We do not want to part from each other in maudlin fashion," he said. I understood what he meant— Yet barely had I yielded to him when quite nearby I heard the most lovely adagio. I was startled. He calmed me by saying that they were nothing but loyal friends, none of whom knew me either personally or by name. What was I to do? I let them finish the adagio.

After N——'s departure, country life lost its charm for me. We hastened back to the capital. Nothing is more tedious than deception after the motivation that inspired and guided it has died out. The role I then had to play was made more arduous, for one thing, by the fact that my husband (who had been totally deceived by N——) imagined in all seriousness that I had returned to him with all my heart and, secondly, because an illness that befell him at this time imposed upon me a whole new burden. By that I mean the duty of having to be constantly at his side caring for him. Cut off from all social contact, I had the greatest struggle trying to endure my life. Our physician was an elderly man known in every quarter to be the greatest misogynist. The abruptness with which he treated me turned me even more against him, and since his removal was the only way to ease my situation, I did not rest until V—— decided to replace him with a young man whose Grecian physiognomy and towering figure were as much a sensation as the art with which he cured all ailments with the simplest of means, according to whether the diseases were sthenic, asthenic, or asthenic-sthenic in nature. I had heard much of this adherent to the Brownian method, but I had not seen him.[24] When he came to see us, his fine appearance spoke so well for his art that I was enchanted by him at once. If the terminology of the Brownians has any sense, then my husband's ailment was a case of genuine asthenia. The doctor himself declared it to be so and prescribed a diet of raw ham and arrack. I cannot deny that these stimulants did their work by getting my husband back on his feet again in short order, albeit not so completely that there did not occur the occasional relapse. But this at first made me think his case might be an asthenic-sthenic one; and no sooner had I told the doctor what I suspected than, guessing my true intent, he complimented my keen insight and insisted that this was at present his view of my husband's condition as well. In any case, a prolonged cure was called for,

[24] The narrator is referring here and in the ensuing pages to the ideas of John Brown (1735–88), a Scottish physician whose theory held life to be the result of continuous stimulation, brought about by such factors as heat, food, emotions, and movement. Disease was therefore caused either by a lack of stimuli (asthenic diseases, treated with strong doses of stimulant drugs) or by an excess of stimuli (sthenic diseases, treated with counterstimulants).

and I had time and opportunity to develop a good rapport with our new doctor.

Platonism in love, as I have always noted, is a trait to which doctors are less inclined than are men of any other class—and this for good reasons, the enumeration of which now would lead us too far afield. Our physician in particular hadn't the slightest notion of this Platonism either. Thus as soon as I had given him to understand in only the most covert way that my husband's asthenia was bound up with great privation for me, he was immediately prepared to provide me with all the recompense I could desire. You can imagine that my husband did not lose by this arrangement, at least not with respect to the regular visits and the longer stays they occasioned—an attentiveness with which the young doctor won over my husband all the more, as doctors in the capital, and especially those with an extensive practice, are ever in hasty flight, which does not allow them to see an individual patient for longer than a few minutes. In addition, while the doctor himself was the veritable personification of the degree of sthenia that constitutes a state of complete health, I was no less than his equal in that respect. We found such pleasure in each other that we arranged provisionally to enter upon a still closer relationship in the event that my husband's asthenic-sthenic condition were to give way to that absence of stimulation commonly known as death. In order not to make my husband suspicious of me, I would take care to alternate between going to meet him when he came from the doctor's and accompanying him there; my time in the anterooms was the most interesting part of my visits to the doctor.

Meanwhile my husband's illness was becoming so prolonged that he was losing his patience. Whatever I did to soothe him, I would achieve my purpose for only a very short time. Then all at once he told me he had need of no doctor if it was possible to be healed by medicine such as I was giving him; and before I was able to stop it, the doctor's bill was settled, and the doctor was dismissed. This move was so sudden that I had to believe my husband had once again become suspicious or, more likely, had been put on the right track by someone.

Since his condition was not so bad that he was unable to carry out any of the activities his office demanded, yet serious enough to necessitate that he refrain from doing any writing himself, he had taken on a secretary to whom he would dictate his letters. He was so dictating one winter evening when the doctor made an unexpected visit, which was intended less for the patient than for the patient's healthy wife. I myself was not a little surprised by it, but I didn't let any fear of being observed keep me from accompanying the doctor as he left. As we tarried in the anteroom to tend to the matter of his payment, it happened that my husband's secretary, their business just concluded, suddenly walked in on us. He had certainly not intended to surprise us, for he had opened the doors to the intervening rooms so loudly and taken so little care to muffle the sound of his footsteps that had we not wanted to be disturbed, he would not have barged in on us. With my presence of mind I made what I could of the situation; yet I was then so foolish as to treat the innocent man—whom I should have tried to win over by treating him in a friendly manner—so disdainfully as to turn him against me, no matter how much he had behaved in every way to give me to understand that he thought no less of me as a result of the incident. It is possible that my husband, guided by his secretary's hints, no longer wanted to play the fool in the piece and thus put an end to a mode of treatment that in any case could have no success.

In any case, a considerable change occurred in my husband's attitude towards me; this was evident from every aspect of his behavior. Of course he never said it outright, but a certain bitterness in his every look, word, and gesture said quite clearly that we had been trying to cure him to death. The whole matter was too delicate to permit discussion. I could do nothing but play ingenuous in the hope of dispelling this delusion, and I did everything in my power to achieve this goal; yet I soon saw that the idea had taken firm root in V——'s mind. By and by it came to the point where I shared his bitterness.

In an unhappy marriage animosity has exactly the same character that it has in the relationships between great powers: at the start there are minor skirmishes, and these continue until the mounting passions result in a major conflict and upheaval. We had had our share of barbed exchanges until finally I declared I had enough of living in a relationship in which I could never be happy; my youthful years would pass me by amid naught but bitter feelings; I would look to a future that could not promise me happier days; each day would increase the tension I would have to bear for many years yet to come; here there could be no solution but—*a divorce*. The dreadful word was spoken, accompanied by a flood of tears; not that I hadn't spoken in earnest, but rather because tears are a kind of extra gift from which we women, by dint of the female glandular system, are unable to refrain. I was counting too strongly on the passion I had awakened in my last lover not to wish gladly to separate from my husband, to whom I could not be true and whose weakness I found increasingly contemptible.

V—— listened to my speech calmly and did not reply right away. After I had waited in vain for a quarter hour for an answer, I had no choice but to leave the room in which this scene had occurred. After a few hours I returned; and when V—— asked me if I had been at home, I answered with steady voice that I had been bringing my affairs into a temporary state of order, because I was firmly resolved to sever the bond that until now had tied me to him.

"So we are to go through with an actual separation?" he asked.

"Nothing less," was my response.

"And in fact because I, an ailing man, have lost my good humor? Is that fair? Can you defend that in any way? Is that worth all the trouble inextricably bound up with a divorce? Your good name must have become a matter of great indifference to you if you can act so frivolously."

I was not prepared for this turn, and still more greatly did the benign expression with which my husband spoke these words affect me.

"You can rely on the fact," he went on, "that I shall never agree to a divorce, no matter what consequences I might have to face as a result. You have always known me until now as an obliging husband; you will come to know me as a very obstinate one when it comes to defending my principles."

"But these principles—" I broke in.

"They are mine, if not those of the world."

What could I do? In such a situation, a rapid reconciliation was the only sensible strategy. I seized upon it, assuming as I did so an expression that made me look as if I were gradually coming to my senses. But in order not to lose advantage completely, I laid down the terms of our peace. Above all I demanded unlimited trust as absolutely necessary for the prevention of renewed conflict. This was granted. The second condition was that I would have to be allowed to entertain or go visiting twice a week, so that I would not suffer a complete lack of pleasant diversion. To this too he consented. As a third point I demanded, for the restoration of my health (which I now alleged to have suffered greatly over the last two years), that I be granted a renewed visit to the spa. This last point encountered little objection since my husband saw such a journey to be to his advantage as well. I would also have liked to make my fourth condition the reinstatement of the Brownian as our family physician, but considering the entire matter seriously, I thought such an impertinence would be going too far.

Mighty storms clear the horizon. The prospects of my marriage became rosier than they had been for some time. My husband combined with his obliging nature a high degree of friendliness. I for my part did not receive such compliance without gratitude. We led a life that was, if not pleasant, at least so tolerable that people could still take us to be relatively happy.

I shall regret forever that I let a serious look divert me from the path I had decided to take. How much misery I would have spared myself if I had shown greater resolve! There are things we must not even think lest they become dangerous. Divorce is one of them. Pondering the matter closely, I see no remedy for the unhappiness that must follow upon such a declaration if it is not at once made a reality. If a woman overcomes her feeling of dependence (or the esteem she is supposed to feel for her husband) to the point that she no longer shrinks from saying, I want to be free, then her husband should let no observation keep him from granting her this freedom. A relationship as profound as marriage will tolerate no middling status: it is either very good, or it is very bad. In societies where ennui or even anarchy prevails, tensions between husband and wife are resolved in bloody fashion. That would commonly be the case in life if fear of punishment did not play a role. This fear holds intact many a bond that should be sundered. Hence the great number of unhappy marriages in which partners cause each other so much torment and grief: for when such a delicate relationship is damaged, nothing can make it whole again.

It was my misfortune that with the convictions that I had already acquired and that I was no longer able to master, I was lacking only one thing—namely a passion such as I had never known, a passion that pursues its goal blindly and that, encountering chasms that it cannot circumvent, leaps them at risk of life and limb. Precisely this passion grew in me, and so gradually that it had confused my mind before I knew how powerful it was. Since this is where the most important period of my life begins, I must now proceed with the greatest possible care and detail so as to pass over in silence nothing that can contribute to the description of my character. I begin my story with myself.

I had reached the age of twenty-seven years, and even though the first bloom of youth had passed, I had not yet completely lost the radiance of my beauty. A certain fullness of figure, instead of contributing to my width, was well suited to my greater height. Bound up with it was a freshness we encounter only in those people who do not lack the means to satisfy their passions. My own passions had developed without harming anything about me. My whole being was likable and pleasing. A pretty mouth, gleaming white teeth, and a voice of rarely encountered beauty would have made me appealing to that sex a woman prefers to please even if my mind had been less felicitously developed than it was. But I grasped far more than women usually grasp; and in truth I may add: more than I may have seemed to grasp. My mode of conversing was always suited to the persons with whom I happened to be dealing; and the agility or cunning of my intellect was so great that I was able at once to master their entire body of ideas as long as they weren't too alien to my own; for although I was not exactly ignorant, I had in fact never concerned myself with actual matters of learning and erudition, since I had always felt that all matters that could lead in any way to pedantry had to be left to the male sex. With an exhaustive grasp of no one topic, I could speak, with as much ease as precision, about all matters pertaining to a woman's sphere of ideas; and if in the ideas themselves there is nothing either lofty or lowly, nothing either grand or petty, and if only the quantity of ideas and the way they are combined determine intellect, then I can say without exaggeration that I was an intelligent woman—and that I was considered to be one by all my acquaintances. If I lacked anything at all, it was what is customarily called sensibility. By that I understand the respect for social relationships that enables people to remain conscientiously within the circle marked out for them and to stifle from the outset desires that cannot be satisfied. After such an admission I scarcely need go on to say that I continued to nurture within me my desire to have a child and that the thought of not fulfilling the destiny of a woman I found all the more unbearable the more highly I esteemed myself in all other respects.

The life I was leading after the most recent conciliation with my husband I found, as I said, to be quite bearable. Renouncing love affairs because I was beginning to find them annoying and frustrating, I now sought pleasure—or at least diversion—in social company; and since I no longer found my pleasure in the purely women's circles I had attended previously, I entered into the mixed circles, in which those of the male sex played the dominant role. I can tell you that I found general acceptance but that I did not conquer. How true is the observation that seduction must be intended if it is to succeed. More than six months passed in this manner. I was as satisfied with my husband as he was with me; we entertained no expectations of each other beyond those that are easily fulfilled and without the fulfillment of which it is impossible to live on good terms.

During this time, a distant relative of my husband had settled in the capital and made our acquaintance. His name is not important, and so I shall call him by his initial. This S—— struck me at the outset as anything but seductive for a woman of my temperament and mind. His best feature was his figure. No man could have been more perfectly built, and no male face could have more appealingly combined the expressions of strength and gentleness. But this Antinous incarnate seemed a body without soul.[25] His every movement was slow; even in his speech this slowness prevailed, except that then there was something more of a solemnity to it. Passion had never found its way to his breast; he seemed capable at most of interest in a hobby, as long as it was something harmless. In a word (and assuming that our times allow a grand image): he resembled the Pacific Ocean, which, since it is moved by no storm, always retains its calm surface. As attractive as his blue eyes were, they were still a

[25] The original's "Antinousfigur" refers to Antinous (also Antinoös) of Bithynia (c. 110–30), who became a member of the entourage of Emperor Hadrian and ultimately his protégé, possibly his lover. After his mysterious drowning in the Nile, he was proclaimed by the grieving emperor to be a god, and his beauty was commemorated in artworks and on coins.

sign of such unconquerable torpor that the mere sight of them was enough to make a person give up any thought of trying to make his languid blood flow any faster. To arrive at a complete picture of S——, imagine a degree of portliness that would be quite unusual for a person of twenty-five (for he could be no older than that) and that promises a later life of excessive corpulence.

With S——'s striking me in this way, I had no trouble remaining true to my resolutions; and since a woman cannot very well avoid asking herself whether a relationship might be possible with this man or that man, I told myself most emphatically that S—— could as little be available for me as I was for him. I saw him at least once every week, but my judgment of him remained the same. Several months passed in this way. I was most firmly convinced that in this territory I had no more discoveries to make beyond the ones I had made at first glance. He was of interest to me as a relative; but he did not interest me as a man or as a human being. What I felt for him was scarcely more than indifference.

During this time, S—— gradually began, after having long cast me into the same class as all other women, to differentiate me from those others. This was apparent from an attentiveness that, without betraying the least sign of passion, showed very clearly that the female sex in its entirety was present for him only in me. At first I did not notice this honor he was according me; but when

I could no longer help but notice it, I discovered in it so much that was fine and selfless that I had to admit to myself that I had done my relative an injustice in my judgment of him. I admit that I did not remain insensitive and that I wished to myself that this man who idolized me might also approach me with his feelings. But he kept himself at such a distinct distance from me and gave so little sign of desiring any more than the purest reverence that I had no choice but to remain for my part within the bounds of propriety. In a quite undefinable way he exerted a commanding power over me, for when I read in his eyes how well he thought of me, I felt the need to live up to the ideal image he had created. What might possibly have become of me if S——, under happier circumstances than mine had been from the very moment of my birth, had become my first lover!

If ever a man of twenty-five years of age had been a novice in love, it was S——, but this in so unusual a way as to make him different from any other novice. When did a novice ever play the commanding role! Yet S—— had such command and—what is an indisputable fact—such command over me! All this while I could remain quite calm, for I knew from so many experiences that feeling is an emotional state that ceases to change and develop only when it dies out. This was something about which S—— knew nothing, and precisely that gave me the advantage. Thus against his will he had to become closer to me than was his original intention. Yet even as he became closer to me, our relationship remained, aside from the reduced distance between us, the same as ever. No contact at all, of even the most innocent kind! Not a word of friendship or love! No wish other than to be near me and exchange ideas with me! No other intention than to feel life more strongly in himself from being near the object of his affections. And all that gave him an expression of utmost benevolence and of a devotion that, enchanting even in the most unattractive face, in his took on an irresistible power.

Such a delicate relationship even the most minor and forgivable misstep can destroy. I was all the more careful, the more my interest grew from day to day. Responding to kindness with kindness, I did not show the slightest trace of devotion, with an expression giving to understand that duty and obligation simply prevented me from doing so. We often went walking in the company of my husband, and although I was not accustomed to letting him guide me, I nevertheless took his arm simply in order to avoid contact with S——. No frivolous word passed my lips, and even though on occasion, when carried away by a good mood or, more often, by my own natural high spirits, I would break into a merriment and laughter out of all proportion to the circumstances at hand, I would nevertheless soon regain my serious demeanor so as not to spoil the situation. Whether we were alone or in the company of my husband, I took the greatest care to avoid anything that could be taken to reveal my feelings towards this man. I had by and by deviated from my usual orbit to such an extent that I felt a stranger to myself and posed myself the naive question of how this strange tension would end. Fate itself intervened to cut the knot.

I had gone to the park with S—— and my husband when, as we were returning, a horse running wild with its rider bore down upon us in so menacing a manner as to cause me, seized by terror, to let go of my husband's arm and, jumping all too incautiously to the side, to fall to the ground, striking my face. S——, beside himself in response to this accident, at once sprang to my aid and lifted me up. In his arms I felt no pain and exhibited a composure that was anything but affected. As I was bleeding from two wounds, my husband hurried away at once to fetch a wagon that was standing nearby, leaving me with S——. S—— did all he could to help me and, when the wagon arrived, lifted me in. I asked him to sit down beside me, and, blushing, he did so. We arrived in front of our house, and he, having once become my protector, now had to help me up the stairs and then look on as my wounds were bandaged. Now it was time for him to depart, and as he wished me a good night, I extended him my hand for the first time, which he could not decline to kiss and with which I thanked him for his help with a gentle squeeze. How much this day had granted me in exchange for a few minor wounds!

When S—— visited us again the following day, I discovered the effect of my handclasp in such an unmistakable manner, from the glow of his eyes, that I could tell myself with the greatest of certainty that many protective layers had been shed from his heart in the course of a single night. Of course it was no more than a brief flight of free thinking that I sensed about his whole bearing, but it was free thinking nonetheless. This discovery gave me immeasurable pleasure, for I now might hope he would go further. Never had I seen him more animated; everything about him was feeling; he could look upon nothing with indifference; hate and love would alternate from one moment to the next in a foolish way. Whatever feelings he might have nurtured for me before, he now *loved* me.

As soon as I was sure of the matter, the most important thing for me was an open declaration, and since it was not permissible for me to force one out of him, I attempted to draw it out of him by cunning. My husband had a younger sister, a girl of eighteen who was, though by no means ugly, still more talented than pretty. This young girl I often invited to visit me, but most of all during the time when I was tending to my wounds within my own four walls. S—— saw her as often as he came to visit, and while the restrictions that her presence put upon him made his feelings for me all the deeper, I intensified this effect even more by according her such praise as to give the appearance that I was aiming at making him my brother-in-law. And what I had intended with this soon came to pass. S——, whose honorable character eschewed all hypocrisy and half feelings, broke off his visits to us and did not appear again until he was expressly invited. My sister-in-law had in the meantime disappeared from our home. Politeness required that he inquire about her, and this opportunity I used to shower her again with praise. S—— countered that I was carrying my partisanship too far.

"So you're not interested in my sister-in-law?" I asked with a smile. He blushed.

"Indeed," I went on, "I would like to become acquainted with the girl whom you will one day make happy with your hand."

S—— answered me most drily that girls were all too silly for him to be able to love one of them.

As little positive as there was to this response, I nevertheless found it most pleasing for the moment, for I needed only to imagine silliness to be a kind of porosity of mind and counter it in my own behavior with a solid sensibility of bearing, and then, considering S——'s indifference to all other women, I would have what I wished, even though the form of the relationship still left something to be desired. Indeed my joy was so great that I didn't even know myself how I should reveal it to him. I continued chatting with him while at times hanging my head in silence, until S—— had no idea at all what he was to do with me and left me to pursue my thoughts alone. After he departed, I was so restless I didn't know what to do. I felt too hemmed in. I went and sat at the window to get some fresh air, then I cast myself on the sofa to concentrate again on my feelings. The distracted state in which I found myself lasted through the evening, and I was sleepless all through the night. The restraint I had imposed on S—— had its effect on me as well. I had never known such a state.

Several weeks passed without anything occurring to bring us closer together, when my husband, quite unexpectedly, learned he was to be transferred, with an advancement in title and salary, to a distant city in the provinces. He had received no official word on this yet; but the minister in whose department he was working had given him preliminary notice that he would propose his name and added that if he were otherwise agreeable, the matter could involve no difficulties. With that, it was all up to me, for my husband no longer cared about anything beyond his professional activity and was pleased to leave me to decide whether we wished to continue living in the capital or not. Had the whole suggestion been made at any other time—that is, in different circumstances than those in which I now found myself—I would have opted for the capital with no further debate. At present I found the matter more complex—and not on its own account but rather where S—— was concerned. I assumed that in spite of the independence in civil matters that his great fortune afforded him, he would not follow us, and I wished to find out whether he would be able to bear the separation from me. Thus after I told my husband that I would take the matter under consideration, I had S—— encounter me while I was deep in thought. When he asked what was troubling me, I did not answer until I had made it look as if I had gathered my full composure. Then I told my friend what was in the works and asked his opinion. He fell silent at once; and after he had paced back and forth a few times in the room we were in, he suddenly departed, assuring me as he did so that I should soon see him again. Indeed he was not gone for more than two hours. His expression was not so cheerful that it would have been taken as completely untroubled, yet he was trying to look cheerful. Efforts of this kind generally fail. Our conversation faltered every few moments, and when, after he had tormented himself and me along with him for long enough, I reminded him of our pending separation, he leapt to his feet as if stabbed and departed again, except that this time, as he left, he pressed into my hand a note that read as follows:

> I have pondered everything. You must go. It would be irresponsible if some consideration not directly connected to your duty or dictated by it were to hold you

back. I cannot follow you, but you will forever remain unforgettable to me.

S——

It was something akin to ecstasy I felt as I read this short note. For what do rank and increased income weigh against the happiness of being loved by a man who has such feelings? Decisive now was merely that I justify my decision in his eyes in a way that would not make me appear to have sacrificed the first of all duties for an interesting affair. Accordingly, I informed him the next day that a more exact calculation of the moving costs and the inconvenience of relationships in a new office had made my husband decide to stay in the capital and that that was to my liking, as I thought too modestly of myself to believe I would remain unforgettable to him. This was the absolute truth, although the decision not to move to the provinces originated with me. S——, who could not know this, tried to remain calm upon hearing this information, but the joy radiating from his eyes betrayed him all too much, and even on that very evening he declared to me in the most naive way in the world that he believed he could no longer live happily without me.

From this moment on, our mutual affection was declared. Passion acts most intensely upon those who have not yet known it; but it need only take on a new form to conquer those as well who imagine they are a match for it. I recall that on this evening I wounded my finger with a sharp penknife, which, heaven knows why, I was holding in my hand. My finger bled freely, and scarcely had S—— seen the blood than he caught it in a wineglass that had been on a side table, added some wine, and drank it off, saying:

"Thus do I swear eternal love!" I was deeply moved by this show of tenderness.

"I wish to do no less than you," I exclaimed, my voice steady. S—— gave me a meaningful look.

"I am completely serious," I repeated. At once, S—— bared his arm, cut himself with the same knife, let his blood trickle into the same glass, and, after he had added some wine, gave it to me. I drank it off with the same words and, with that, pressed a glowing kiss upon the lips of my friend.

You will now expect that one barrier after another fell away at this point. Had S—— not been involved, that would undoubtedly have been the case. From what I had come to know of him, even the most proper girl could not be more proper than he. I would have had to dare the first move, and I was too much a woman to do that. Instead of declaring his intentions, he merely glowed, and this glow was at once so intense and so cautious that it consumed all desire. I bade that he might now address me with the informal "you" when we were alone together.

"No," he answered, "I wish to continue foregoing this

pleasure; and besides, I shall better master my passion if I continue to address my lady friend with the formal 'you.'" I asked him soon after that if he would stay with me a while longer.

"I must rest," he responded. "Allow me to leave; from now on we shall see each other every day." And with that he hurried away.

When on the following day he came to me again, he was more serious than I had ever seen him, and after he had finally mustered the necessary courage, he addressed me in the following manner:

"We have entered into a relationship that, if I rightly judge our characters, we perhaps should not have come to know for some time yet. Anticipations of this kind must necessarily bring unhappiness. If one is virtuous, they are a torment; if one is not virtuous, they ultimately lead to self-disdain. For my part, I am not inclined to become untrue to the principles that have guided me to this point in my life. I most solemnly renounce all displays of favor and affection that run counter to the rights of your spouse, and I lay claim to no more than friendship in the most proper sense of the word. How difficult it is to remain cold towards the woman one loves I never felt so strongly until yesterday. The decision I have made today in order to give strength to my frailty may sound like it is from a fanciful novel; but it is the only one I was able to make. We cannot both reside in the same city; we cannot, considering the mood we are now in, even exist in the same country; for since we do not lack the means to overcome the distance between us, we shall be inclined to seek each other's company if our separation is not so great. We must be seas apart. I have for some time now been wanting to go to England. This I shall now do. As long as V—— lives, our relationship can never be a legal one.— Perhaps he will outlive us both. The best we can do is not assume that this will be so. Should he die, I shall return to you at once; but in any case I shall return in three years. You can do no other than to accept my resolve as right."

Had there been anything laughable about S——, I would have laughed at this novel-like declaration; yet still he had power over me, as always. Since he had made his decision—and precisely this decision bespoke a way of thinking that people cannot but respect—it was impossible for me even to presume to go against it, for then I would have ended our relationship once and for all. So I had no choice but to attempt to undermine it. I assumed an expression of dejection and told him that his resolve corresponded to the idea I had of his magnanimity and that to hinder him from carrying it out would be something I could not attempt without coming to despise myself. Yet I asked that he might consider what would become of me if he were to carry out this resolve at once, since a feminine heart had not the strength of a masculine one, and that I could thus predict I would not be able to bear a sudden parting. To this S—— responded by asking me how long he should stay. I requested six months.

"That is too long," he answered. "In such a span of time even the firmest resolve could be shaken." We negotiated until he consented to remain in the capital for three months. But in doing so, he imposed the dreadful condition that he would not see me during this time other than in the company of my husband. I was about to tell him that this would make my husband completely unbearable to me, yet where are we to find the courage to make such an admission if virtue is forced upon us and we are of half a will to obey?

There the matter remained. S—— visited daily. I accustomed myself all the more easily to the obligation he imposed upon me because I saw he was having trouble holding to his intentions. For if the conversations in V——'s presence were anything but interesting, there were certain small satisfactions that only lovers know how to cherish and that can take the place of the greater pleasures they must renounce. V—— was treated by S—— with the greatest respect, which grew precisely in proportion to his becoming better acquainted with him. Not seldom did I feel S—— was reproaching himself for deceiving such a fine man. This was a feeling that I could not permit myself to express and that I nevertheless had to treat with the greatest consideration if I was not to betray myself. The only way out I could find was to enhance my worth in S——'s eyes still further, and I succeeded in doing so by appearing to become more and more calm and composed.

All this while the time for our separation was approaching inexorably. How quickly three months pass at a loved one's side! S—— remained so calm that at times I had to think all his passion for me had died. Yet my own heart was beating so intensely that I had no end of trouble hiding the anxiety that tormented me constantly. So little had the long preparation achieved its purpose that my passion for S—— had only grown more powerful. The thought of our separation was unbearable. I pondered ways in which I could hinder it; but I found none but such as could only postpone it, and I told myself that my state could not be improved by postponements. In a kind of despair I resolved to attack S—— directly, but this maenad could not vanquish her Orpheus.[26] His resolve remained unshaken, and I endured the shame of having fallen out of my role.

I am as little able to describe the indescribable as anyone; but I can say in general that my state came very close

[26] The maenads were the maniacal women of Greek mythology who slew the aloof Orpheus. After his failed attempt to rescue Euridice from the underworld, he sang his complaints and spurned the Thracian maidens who wished to captivate him. Excited by the rites of Bacchus, they attempted to kill him, succeeding only when their frenzied screaming drowned out his saving music and they could tear him limb from limb.

to madness and that the need to conceal it intensified my torment more than a little. Imagine, if you can, a woman for whom only one mode of existence is possible and who is forcibly held back from such an existence. You know the story of Sappho. Think of that woman as, driven by her burning passion up onto the Leucadian cliff, she is about to cut short her long torment by her resolute plunge into the waves of the sea. Had I been imprisoned in a cloister, with S—— standing in the moonlit night outside my cell, I, like that Sarmatian damsel whose name I have forgotten, without fail would have plunged from the third story into his arms.[27] I would do anything to gain possession of him, but all my powers left me at the thought of seeing him depart. Tears were my only relief.

In such a state, one morning after a sleepless night of wild torment, I went to my escritoire looking for something—I no longer recall what—and as I opened one drawer after another, I caught sight of the poison that gave rise to such a strange scene between my father and me and that, upon his death, I took with me lest it fall into the wrong hands. Since then I had not thought back upon it. To see it again was to feel my entire body start

[27] The Sarmatians were a nomadic tribe known since the fifth century BC, by legend descended from Scythian fathers and Amazon mothers. From the first century AD they were documented in Eastern Europe and Ukraine, ranking among the tribes threatening the weakened Roman Empire. The editors of this volume could not trace the story of the Sarmatian damsel and her leap for love.

to tremble. I never find it surprising that there were once times—and that there are still places on earth—in which people saw a thought that could be born only of the most intense passion as the inspiration of an evil demon; for in order not to commit such an act, one must be in firm mental control of oneself, which is difficult at all times and, in a state of passion, nearly impossible. Something like that I might well have said about myself in the moment the poison caught my eye, so suddenly did the decision come upon me to make use of it and, along with it, the fear of the ruin that the execution of that decision, in the event of its discovery, would bring in its wake. A cold sweat bathed my limbs. I struggled to make my way to the nearest sofa. For some time I was as if devastated. My breast was torn by a mighty struggle. I fought with myself like a woman in despair. My entire state was worthy of pity, and yet no relief was possible.

Morality does not exist for a mind in turmoil, for a mind in which the storm of passion is raging. In vain I sought out anything that could bring me back from this black resolve; the only answer to all the objections that I posed to myself was: "S—— is at stake, and you will lose him forever if you part with him." It was as if no power in the world was strong enough to suppress the thought once it had seized control of me. The fear disappeared in the same measure that I pondered the means to put that thought into action. "What recourse," I asked myself, "does your sex have other than cunning, since nature and society have conspired to deprive it of power? What for a man would be a crime is not one for a woman. The laws—what are they but tyrants to be evaded? And is it your fault that you are forced to purchase your freedom with such means? Did you yourself not propose a divorce, and was it not denied you? Does any recourse remain? The utmost integrity on your part would be the utmost foolishness."

My inner turmoil had not yet subsided when S—— came to pay me a visit. It was an exception to the rule that he himself had prescribed; but since he had not failed to notice the state I had been in for some days, he considered it necessary, as he told me himself, to impart to me some calming words of comfort. In the glory of a god he stood before me. Everything he said assuaged my impetuousness. If what was going on within me had been gentler in nature, I would have fallen down before him and prayed to him. Now I adopted an expression as if I could be led back to reason. I admitted my weakness and promised to be steadfast; I even gave him my hand on it, saying that the example of his strength would surely not remain without effect upon me. He sat down beside me and began to speak of the future we faced, a future of which he painted for me an all too attractive picture without sensing in the least that I was envisioning it in my mind's eye in far more radiant colors. His eyes were alight with joy.

"We shall become happy," he said, "if we deserve to be so, and such happiness we can earn only through devotion."

Unfortunately, this devotion did not at all suit my intense temperament, which caused me to consider only the present. Scarcely had S—— left than my resolve returned with doubled strength, as my nature turned his balsam into poison. I was pondering now only how I would act my part in such a way as to evade even the falcon's eye of love. Too much calm would be no good; too much passion would be worse still. Of those two elements I would have to compose my behavior and indeed do so in such a way as to appear to have given in to the requests of my friend. My husband had to believe that he had become more than ever the object of my attention. But most of all the blackness of the deed itself would have to shield me from any suspicion, and that required me to commit it under such circumstances that it would become ten times blacker than it was by its very nature.

Thus I was firmly resolved to take possession of my beloved by poisoning my husband. To do this I chose V——'s birthday, which was drawing near. When that day arrived, I summoned up all my cheerfulness. In order to prevent any inclination to weakness, I had taken the precaution of inviting S—— to breakfast, then a larger company of acquaintances and friends for the midday meal. Of S——'s presence I had need in order, by seeing him, to strengthen my will to carry out the deed; the latter gathering I required to create a diversion both for him and for me when the first effects of the poison manifested themselves. After S—— arrived, we sat down to our breakfast. I had not the courage to shake the poison into the first cup I handed my husband. But I had to bring myself to poison the second cup, because I knew that his tendency to moderation might make him decline the third. At this point, fate was about to play a trick on me that would have struck me dead on the spot had I not had the presence of mind to divert it at the last moment. V—— and S—— were sitting side by side on the sofa, caught up in a lively conversation. I was standing before them, my heart beating, when suddenly I noticed that S—— was taking my husband's cup and about to drink it down. Like an electric shock it shot through my every limb, and I was on the verge of revealing the whole secret when I then suddenly summoned the full strength of my will to inform S—— that he had taken my husband's cup and thus set right the fatal error. My husband soon drank what was meant for him. The deed was done.

The company gathered an hour later. We sat down at the table. I seemed to be occupied only with serving them; but all my attention was riveted on my husband. His nausea began right after the soup course, and soon it became so bad that he was forced to leave the company. I accompanied him into the adjoining room and left him to be looked after by one of the servants. To our company I excused the matter by saying he was often prone to these dreadful attacks, and I talked about it as if it were an illness that still lingered on since the last cure and thus was of no significance.

You can well imagine that our guests were not happy to hear this news. Propriety demanded all the more caution, as I could not but rise from time to time in order to go to inquire about my husband's condition. I had done this a few times when I returned, my entire bearing an expression of sorrow, and, when asked about my husband, I responded that his illness had taken a serious turn. The result was that the party broke up earlier than planned, and this was all the more to my advantage, since I had no time to lose in order to make myself master of the situation.

V—— was experiencing the most violent cramps, accompanied by copious vomiting. I had to send the servants away, lest they become suspicious. Necessity was more demanding than ever. I sat down lovingly at the bedside of the patient and simulated a sympathy I did not feel. He demanded a certain doctor. I promised I would have the doctor sent for at once and left to fetch a servant; but not only did I wait until my husband's illness had worsened, I also sent for a different doctor, since I mistrusted the sharp eye of the one my husband had requested. When the doctor arrived, V—— was so weak that he was unable to speak. I spoke for him by describing the symptoms in detail. The pulse that the doctor took was not promising; I could see this from his expression. Bathed in tears, I sat waiting for the doctor's diagnosis. Now of course he tried to calm me with assurances that he was not giving up hope of saving the patient, but I knew all too well what to expect from these assurances to be misled even for a moment. Medicine was prescribed, and so on.

S—— arrived late in the evening to inquire about my husband's condition, a visit that, troublesome in any case, became still more so when he insisted on seeing my husband. I attempted to prevent this; yet when I saw he was adamant in his resolve, I relented—an ill-considered blunder, perhaps. S—— remained so long with my husband that I became impatient. When he finally appeared, he said, his tone curt, "V—— is dying!" And with that he left, without wasting further words.

Now I began to grow fearful. I went back to my husband and would have sacrificed half my life if it could have saved him. I wished in vain! He died a few hours later amid the most horrible pains a guiltless man has ever suffered.

I thought I would despair; and yet I could not give myself over to despair if I did not want to sacrifice myself to disgrace. The doctor whom I had called had departed without any suspicions about me. As soon as V—— died, I sent for him once more in order to learn what I was to think of the faint into which my husband had fallen. The doctor came, and barely did he see the deceased than he said that I must compose myself, for my husband was quite dead.

You can well imagine how I took this admonition and information. Yet my frenzy of grief lasted no longer than until the doctor had left. No matter how much I regretted my act, I had to suppress this regret in order not to betray myself through some thoughtless word or act. Since all our servants were very devoted to my husband, I first of all took care that none of them come close to the corpse. An old woman whom I had come to know several years before by way of my earlier interest in superstition helped me do what had to be done. With much loud lamentation I made known the sudden death of my husband. A funeral service and burial were arranged. In short, everything went so well that no one became suspicious, excepting only him on whose account I had committed the crime.

All the fear I felt at my husband's deathbed immediately after his demise was caused by S——, whose strange behavior at our last parting I did not know how to explain. And still more fearful was I when, even after the burial, he chose neither to visit nor to communicate. I wrote, inquiring how he was, and received the answer that he was very ill. Decency imposed bonds upon me that I could not break. All I could do was inquire every hour until I received word that I would soon hear from him. I felt as if I were being tortured, and still day after day passed without my hearing a word from S——. My impatience had reached its peak when I received the following note, along with a packet:

> All is not as it should be, and what I am suffering I cannot describe. No, I never thought it would end like this; I never dared imagine such a thing. You should know that V—— himself told me he was dying an unnatural death. I have no proof to show you, but when I consider everything that has occurred between us, then I find enough to be convinced that you have committed murder. It is true, you murdered out of love for me; but how can I be grateful for that, since it has happened so against my will? My trust—it is gone forever.
>
> What am I to do? I have sworn to love you eternally. I will keep this promise. Although I am but the cause and not the perpetrator of this murder, I will nevertheless atone for it. In the moment you receive this note, I shall have left the capital, and after twenty-four hours I shall be no more. The accompanying package contains a few precious items that I can pass on only to you.
>
> S——

There seemed now nothing left for me but a violent death. Had ever a woman found herself in such a situation? My misfortune cast me down. Why did I not have the strength to kill myself? How dearly I wished to do so! Ringing my hands, I ran back and forth in my room and cursed my deed and denounced my very existence. All furies possessed my heart and chased me hither and thither.

Bereft of calm and rest, I was nevertheless damned to remain calm. I pictured S—— lying in his own blood, and as if he were lying before me, I plunged to the ground in order that I might breathe out my last breaths of life with him. What a divine figure was dashed and lost with him! And how beautiful, how enviable his death, so in keeping with his sacred life!

"Oh, how well you have acted," I cried out, "not to die close to me! You would only have sullied yourself! How little worthy I was of you! For all my boundless love I was able only to deceive you and drive you to suicide."

Since all this while I did not have the courage to follow in S——'s footsteps; since my grief abated with each day; since, in a word, I found the courage to go on living, I must, before I continue with my confessions, break off here. I am all the more deserving of a pause, since no small struggle is required to call such a life to mind once again. Full of revulsion, I have, from time to time, cast down my pen and crushed it beneath my feet, all the while shedding countless tears. I am a monster, I know it, but I still feel I am a human being.

Third Book

You have seen up to this point the unusual way in which I became a criminal—and perhaps necessarily had to become one.

Before I continue with my confessions—and I have

further significant ones to make to you—I must begin with two comments that people who have made a habit of virtue have no opportunity to deduce. Both contain the key to my ensuing actions; both, unless I am very much mistaken, favor true virtue; both can be misunderstood only by those who adhere to the narrow school definitions of virtue; and both, in unmistakable fashion, add to the general area of human understanding.

The first of my comments is that regret is nothing other than fear of punishment, be this punishment a real or an imagined one. As *real* I denote the punishment that society imposes for certain actions that it terms crimes because they run directly counter to the ultimate goal of social organization; as *imagined* I denote those punishments that people assume will be carried out after this life by some higher judge whom we do not know. Whoever then fears neither the real nor the imagined punishment, such a person I declare to be incapable of regret. In order not to fear real punishment, a person must either be above the law or have taken, when committing the crime, such precautions as to consign the discovery of the crime to the realm of the impossible; not trembling at the prospect of imagined punishment requires only a lack of faith, which poses no difficulties for people capable of crime. Imagine, then, an irreligious person who has evaded the law in one of the ways I have just mentioned—or who believes that he or she has done so—and it will be impossible to imagine that such a person feels regret about the misdeed committed.

My second comment is that for the person who really feels regret there remains no other recourse but to find every possible means of self-escape. We can divide all actions into virtuous and criminal ones. Virtuous actions are those that, while conducive to the individual's private advantage, are at the same time useful to society; criminal actions, by contrast, are those through which one seeks to satisfy one's private advantage only at a cost to society. Once one has allowed oneself to commit a crime and must then, in the possibility that it will be discovered, fear real punishment, one seeks to escape this unpleasant feeling and gradually realizes that the longest sequence of virtuous actions does not suffice to destroy the recollection of the crime. This undoubtedly results from the fact that society punishes the smallest crime but does not reward the virtuous act unless it reap great advantage from doing so. Be that as it may, the fact remains that the criminal, while attempting to flee his own awareness of his guilt and never reaching that goal by means of virtuous deeds, ultimately finds no other recourse but to suppress his unpleasant memories with acts that add to the number of crimes and thus in the end to bring about a confusion that takes the place of a good conscience. As dreadful as this sounds, I know of no stronger proof of the reality of virtue and of its difference from vice, whereas all the modifications that the more complete or the more incomplete social state imposes upon both play no significant role. Since I in particular have found myself in this situation and, moreover, intend my confessions less to excuse my actions than to explain them, I must ask you to remember the idea that a regretful person is ever in search of self-escape and can find such escape only through self-confusion. This is the most important conclusion I am able to draw about myself, and it confirms in a truly human way the old saying that whoever has once given himself to the devil is the devil's forever. And now I shall continue with my confessions.

The news of S——'s death made every wound of my heart bleed anew. I came by it in the public newspapers. They reported it as an unusual case of a traveler of surpassingly beautiful physique and to all appearances in completely good health both physically and mentally, who had, in the hotel at B—— (eight leagues from the capital), taken his life with a pistol shot, and they asked any and all of his relatives to inquire and apply regarding the deceased's inheritance. That S—— would keep his promise I was certain from his previous behavior; I knew him too well to think him capable of making an empty threat. Still, the verification of his death cast me down anew. Thus was my entire life's plan torn to shreds forever, and nothing of my expectations remained to me other than the thought of one murder committed and a suicide caused by it, of two men who were worthy of the best fate. Especially S—— and his gentle conscientiousness tormented me. Without his discovery of the murder and its tragic results, I would have remained at peace, and I would have been completely his—I cannot imagine even now that I would have been unhappy at his side. Thus his loss was the only thing I truly mourned; but since I could not avoid thinking back to the cause of that loss, I also wept for my husband, and in fact all the more bitterly, the more S—— had made me aware of my guilt. It is difficult to find one's way out of a persistent confusion of complex feelings. I am portraying myself as accurately as I can recollect; and what I can say as a certain truth is that I have no intention of portraying myself and my situation more to my advantage.

For several weeks I had left unopened the packet I had received from S—— with his last letter. When I finally opened it, it was more boredom than curiosity that drove me to act; for how could all the treasures his note had promised me replace what I had lost in his person? Yet I found, in addition to all the precious items, in the narrower sense of the word, several banknotes that put me in possession of considerable sums of money. Should I state the unadorned truth? The less I had counted on making such a discovery, the more pleasure it gave me. People might think of me what they will, but the fact is I felt that life took on a greater worth for me with my having attained the basic means of making it sweeter, namely wealth. The vanity that likely never completely dies out in any female heart now reasserted itself in mine. I thought of a larger entourage than I had had before, of finer furniture, even of exquisite jewelry. S——'s generosity was all the more welcome to me in the light of how my own fortune had shrunk, with the result that aside from the modest pension I drew from the widows' fund, I had retained very little.

I also thought of entering once again into the great world of society. As dear as S—— had been to me, I still had not given up all social contacts for his sake. For taking them up again as a widow, I could discern no better means than seeking out once more my old acquaintances through whom I had first entered that sphere. You may easily guess that I am speaking here of none other than ——d and the ——ks and their following, with whom I was once again on good footing. They were all the better suited to my purpose since I was resolved to further my sure social standing still more by exhibiting an inspiring degree of sorrow.

I do not know from my own experiences whether human blood is as interesting a sight as some people claim; but I do know that human tears capture the interest of those who have not become insensitive to them as a result of their own misfortune. This is especially the case with elderly spinsters. The heartfelt intensity with which they set about offering condolences to the bereaved can have no other purpose than coaxing forth tears and taking pleasure at the sight of them; for if such an intent were not involved, they would not concern themselves with condolences. How many women I now encountered were bent upon singing my late husband's praises! All had known him only by sight or *par renommée*, as they say, but how could that detract when the important thing was learning how a widow felt? Their wish was fulfilled at least insofar as I let there be no lack of tears. I need not tell you that they flowed in memory of S——; for a man whom one has dispatched with poison one can hardly mourn with tears, since hypocrisy does have its limits and certain feelings cannot be mutually exchanged. People were satisfied with my tears, inasmuch as in this world people always go by the effects without tracing them back to their causes. At first they called me a woman of great feeling; then they took pleasure in comforting me as if I were making too much of my pain; finally they came to the point of avoiding conversing about anything that could remind me of my loss.

In the eyes of the world I had played my role well enough to extricate myself from even the merest shadow of suspicion; but how was I to escape the memories that always led me back to S——? I cannot describe the torment I felt whenever I thought back to the heaven that I had wanted to create for myself and that had been torn from me as if by a stroke of magic. Unbearable seemed the void I felt within myself; incessantly I sought what was no longer possible for me to have. I resolved to leave the home in which I had committed murder; but I lacked the courage to carry out that resolve, so painfully sweet were the memories that bound me to that dwelling. And all my talents, too, were being submerged by this one feeling. I thought I might find some distraction in reading, but what ideas would have had the strength to replace those images that were ever present before my mind's eye? No matter how much I forced myself, I read and read without being aware of what I had read. And in like manner, things I was told, unless they bordered on the horrible, would go echoing past my ears. I believe I was the only female creature in all Europe who was not moved to hear about the events of the Reign of Terror in France, who felt more joy than regret; for my misfortune occurred at just that time, and I took a kind of satisfaction in learning that there was at least one place on earth where there were people who, driven by conflicting passions, found, as I had done, no other alternative but to commit murder. While this was my prevailing mood, there was not a complete lack of moments when, moved by gentler feelings, I took it to be my duty to atone for my transgression by doing deeds of compassion. Foolish notion! What meaningful effect could I have on all that suffering? I gave alms and did so with a generous hand, but did I give more than I could spare? Did I lose anything through my kindness, and did I gain anything by thinking I was doing good? With such actions the right hand must not know what the left hand is doing; every selfish intent poisons them. Now I began for the first time to realize that the effects of an evil deed cannot be balanced by a good one; for my inner state remained the same, no matter how tirelessly I tried to dispel it by all those good deeds. I felt as if all my prospects of social harmony with other people were at an end and as if I totally lacked the power that, in our contacts with creatures of our own species, we call the power to attract. Naught did I feel within me but the power to repel.

In this mood I could do nothing but try to forget myself as much as possible. I believed I could achieve this by becoming more socially active than I had ever been before. Forcing myself to do this had a beneficial effect at least to the extent that it tired me out. As little command as I had of the jargon that people call conversation, by forcing myself to take part I gradually learned it. I even became so adept as to monopolize conversations. Modest people might often have marveled in silence at the glibness of my tongue; but had they known how a certain unspeakable desperation was contributing to my loquacity, they would have been more inclined to sympathy than to rebuke. I once came to be seated opposite the well-known Colonel A——. The man spoke well, and since he had seen and experienced a great deal, his conversation was even edifying. This time he seemed to outdo himself. A lady commented about it, complimenting the good colonel.

"What makes me so entertaining today, Madame," he responded with great rectitude, "is nothing other than a dull pain I have been feeling in my lower abdomen for several weeks now, which, since it can bode naught but ill for me, I have been trying in every possible way to forget."

Much the same I could have said of myself had I been allowed to show as much rectitude. But fortunately, people seldom attempt to probe the causes of what they see; and to my still greater good fortune my talkativeness so endeared me to the great majority of people—whom we know never to suffer from a surplus of ideas and feelings—that I was welcome everywhere.

Yet this distraction lasted only as long as I found the people with whom I was associating to be interesting novelties. Then the old disgust would emerge anew. To stifle it I would seek out all the diversions the capital had to offer; I intentionally use this term because it best describes my attitude. The concerts I attended bored me in the most unbearable way, and if my self-observations are otherwise accurate, this is because music, as soon as it has had its initial effect, puts people in a state of revery that, while it may be pleasant for innocent people, is very unpleasant for those who are not. Thus Shakespeare's well-known comment about the powers of music is quite right where moral people are concerned;[28] yet instead of inferring too much solely from that view, we should bear in mind that there are people whose greater affinity for the intellectual faculties makes them averse to the state of revery and who thus, even when they are utterly innocent, are apt to flee music, for the reason that they know from experience that it leads only to revery. More interesting by far than the concerts I found the plays, and especially the tragedies. I have already told you how, since my youth, I have had a preference for this mode of theatrical presentation. While at an early age I took pleasure merely in great displays of emotion, I now came to take pleasure in observing the role of necessity in truly tragic events, which often caused me to fault our tragic poets for their less than complete knowledge of their craft. This is not the place for a more thorough explanation of this observation; but I have never been able to understand, for example, how two characters as dissolute and shallow as the prince and his chamberlain in *Emilia Galotti* can bring about a tragic sequence of events; for in order to believe in the veracity of such a character as Marinelli, a person would have to believe, in defiance of the most

[28] The narrator is likely referring here to the lines of the song sung by Queen Katharine in act 3, scene 1, of *Henry VIII*: "In sweet music is such art, / Killing care and grief of heart / Fall asleep, or hearing, die" (Shakespeare, *Complete Works* 2: 1038).

rigid orthodoxy, in inherent sin itself.[29] All nontragic productions I found boring. I would more likely have been able to play a comic role successfully than have taken any pleasure in seeing one. How often, whenever people saw me looking downcast and sad, was I invited to go to see one of the farces in which Herr *** was playing the leading role; but how little this well-meant advice was suited to my situation! A medicine can kill one patient and restore the other to health, according to their differences. The other things besides the theater that gave me pleasure were exhibitions involving dangerous undertakings, such as daring horseback riding—by the so-called English riders—and tightrope walking; but while I was admiring the skills involved, I would think back on all the daring riders, tightrope walkers, and the like who fill our moral world.

A person can add to her daily needs one thing and then the other; but as soon as it becomes habit, she finds herself back where she started. Such was my case in my efforts to forget myself. I reached the point where I found the capital city with all its wonders boring; and since I promised myself much from a journey, I did not hesitate to set off on my way. I enjoyed the excited feeling that came with

[29] *Emilia Galotti* (1772) is a tragedy by Gotthold Ephraim Lessing (1729–81), a German critic, aesthetician, and dramatist who played a major role in the emergence of a German national theater and modern German drama.

traveling, and still more marked was the effect of the incessant change of scene. In order to prolong the resulting cheerfulness, I attempted to enhance the effects of the new and interesting by means of art. Not content with being more keen in my inquiries than I would have been in my normal emotional state, I took to keeping a travel journal in which I wrote down everything remarkable I had seen or heard. Famous scholars, but especially famous writers, I did not fail to seek out; for the more a person can produce in the way of news about such men, whether it speak well of them or ill, the more welcome that person is in a society that counts it to one's credit if one has been face to face with a Klopstock, a Wieland, a Goethe, or such like. With the reception I enjoyed wherever I went I was very pleased; a traveling person's contacts will always go well if he or she has some grasp of the art of treating people in accordance with their personal preferences—an art best practiced by renouncing one's own individuality.

I shall let you imagine to yourself my six months spent in this fashion, for the events of my travels do not belong in my confessions. In addition, I have told you and many others the most important parts on other occasions—and perhaps in greater detail and in more talkative manner than I should have. Since I found no place I liked better than the capital, I returned home. My spirit was indeed refreshed when I arrived back here. People were happy to see me again. I had to tell about all I had done. The experiences I had gathered were varied enough to strike people as sufficiently different from what was being talked about in the capital, and so they listened to me with as much attention as if I had journeyed to China, even though I had gone barely eighty or ninety leagues from where I lived. You know how most women think these days; a person is considered an exotic wonder indeed if she is able to speak about something other than events at court, the most recent masked ball, the most popular actress, and the latest murders done in desperation. Who knows why! For me all this had the fortunate effect of banishing to the nether reaches of my soul certain thoughts that were tormenting me; it also prolonged, save for a few unavoidable relapses, my artfully created mood of good cheer.

Winter was approaching. Fearing its influence on my mood, I was seriously thinking of finding some activity that would occupy my entire attention, when I read in the public newspapers an announcement for a series of lectures on the *Critique of Pure Reason*. Several of my friends had attended the same series the year before and talked to me ad nauseam about space and time, about the amphiboly of the concepts of reflection, about the categories, about the categorical imperative, and so on—all topics I did not understand in the least. Since now I had no low opinion of myself and was just at a loss for some undertaking that might involve all my intellectual abilities, I was happy to subscribe to the series of lectures, because I also saw it as a way to avoid the embarrassment with which I had to resign myself to silence whenever there was talk of the philosopher of Königsberg. So in the tutelage of one of the local philosophers who, in return for money and kind words, rattle off the ideas that an exceptional mind has thought out, I took great pains to probe the depths of metaphysics. The tone in which my teacher spoke of these matters suggested that nothing in the world was clearer than his lecture; I even believe he had an exceptional grasp of Kant. Yet whether it was my fault or that of the topic, I simply could not see the two-times-two-is-four in all these things. I took the liberty of alerting my teacher to the fact that it could be seen in quite a different light; yet on this point he was not about to capitulate. And while he did praise the freedom with which I ventured to be of another opinion, he was more inclined to see some misunderstanding on my part than to yield even one iota of what he assured me he had straight from the mouth of his esteemed teacher himself. Oh, woeful the philosophy people must accept just as they once accepted the edicts of arrogant popes! It was surely not the intention of this philosophy's founder, just as the originators of the Holy Scripture never suspected that Roman bishops would be its spokesmen. I realized that no system, be its object of concern the natural or the spiritual side of mankind, is tenable; for both are destined to undergo changes that absolutely cannot be reckoned in advance. What we call reason is, as all experience shows, nothing but the most advanced state of development that a society has attained in a given span of time and that is manifest in those of its members whom we call philosophers; but to hold this reason within certain bounds or even to attempt to subject it to certain laws seems to me unreason itself, namely the greatest misuse of our power of thought. And unless I am mistaken, there resides simply in the title *Critique of Pure Reason* a contradiction that defies any solution and about which, to the good fortune of all those who make a living from speculative philosophy, very few have even dreamt.

Now I am talking like a learned doctor with a good quantity of furrows on his brow and a still more imposing beard. Where don't our misadventures lead us! The one I have just been talking about at least had the good result of teaching me to cease being deceived by scholarly terminology and of causing me to correct the esteem in which I had previously held the local philosophers and their followers. If only the study of critical philosophy had not been so harmful for me in another respect!

My physical system, from the moment I renounced all love affairs, had undergone a significant change, to the development of which my sorrow over S——'s death had contributed and which the study of critical philosophy seemed then to bring to full bloom. This change consisted in the fact that I had not only lost my previous figure and become broad but also turned so brownish-red of complexion as to dread comparisons to copper, and this change entailed as well a weakening of my sight, which was obviously a result of my incessant reading and writing. What woman likes growing ugly? Philosophy was supposed to distract me, not change my physique. As soon as I realized that the latter was happening in a way that with time would turn me into a monster of ugliness, I began to consult, in addition to my teacher, a physician. As chance would have it, he was completely opposed to philosophical speculation. Barely had I told him about my way of life than he demanded that I hand over to him my *Critique of Pure Reason*, so that, as he said, he could give it away to a spice merchant, and he advised me to cut my notebooks up into sewing patterns.

"If you wish to keep your health," he went on, "and not fall victim to running eyes and pustules of all kinds and ultimately have a mustache, then you must return once again to the diet you gave up. You are still too young to let yourself renounce the joys of love completely. Giving up certain habits all at once is not merely burdensome but even dangerous. Put your faith more in experience than in speculation, for speculation brings us not a step forward but instead makes us chase forever in the same circle." And he went on, with a laugh: "Bear in mind that we live only once and that all grand words are no more than soap bubbles for the amusement of children."

That I was receptive to such advice I scarcely need tell you; my mind was not yet so twisted that I would not prefer what I had learned from experience to anything that was worse. I was almost ashamed of not having come upon such a clever notion myself; for since ultimately only diversion was important to me, I could find it as easily in love affairs as in philosophical speculation.

As I now went on to ponder the matter further, it seemed to me most advisable to aim at a marriage through which I would become what people call a *grande dame*. To be sure, my figure could contribute little to attaining that goal; yet since a goodly portion of men can be captivated by an appeal to an interest other than love, my fortune, for which I had S——'s generosity to thank, was of great usefulness. I could count still further to my credit the fact that one of my aunts who had reached a rather advanced age and was constantly ailing, would not live much longer and that as a result I had the distinct prospect of becoming even more wealthy. I believed I could not fail to make a good match, once I was of a will to do so.

In order in the meantime to make use of the good advice the doctor had given me, I lured into my nets one of the newcomers who make the social rounds as candidates for pastoral office. The young man was far more in need of a parsonage than in need of a bride; but by promising to secure him the former I induced him to put up with doing his best to further the improvement of my complexion's hue. I had cause to be pleased with him. Only one thing displeased me about him, and that was the devotion he had to his fiancée. This devotion was so great that it shone through at every point, and since ultimately even I found it cruel to keep putting off my promise, I turned to a man whom I knew to have very close ties to the Minister of Religion and thus soon had the pleasure of seeing my protégé promoted and given a parish.

He was followed by a second, a third, a fourth. I shall pass over the details in silence, as they all involved a miserable repetition of the same brutality. Liaisons of this kind have much that is burdensome for a woman who has not totally ruined her reputation; for in addition to the fact that such affairs must be initiated with great caution, they demand as well, as long as they go on, further measures to ensure the subsequent discreet silence of the men. That is a task truly not easy to solve. My position was always such as to make myself appear to be more the one seduced than the seductress. In addition I always sought to be of use to my lovers not only with respect to social and professional matters but also by supplying them with money when they needed it. Nothing debases a man more in his own eyes than such acts of social, professional, and financial assistance; and once this debasement is successfully accomplished, then, as a rule, his silence can be relied upon.

In the meantime it had become known I was not disinclined to come once again under the yoke of marriage; and well might I express myself thus, since for me marriage had become a necessary yoke that could be of value in my eyes only insofar as it involved a certain amount of security. In addition, the conditions had become known under which marriage could take place. There was no lack of men who found it worth the trouble to cast a closer look at me. Many of them were ardent in wooing me; but since I could assume with utmost certainty that precisely these men were least suited to fulfilling my conditions, they were also the first whom I dismissed as suitors. As soon as the personalities themselves are not taken into account and the sole concern is the marriage of one considerable fortune with another, a person needs to exert a degree of caution no less than that required for the solution of complex mathematical problems; for the main fear on both sides is and remains the fact that one can be deceived. Once everything has finally been made clear, for widows of property there remain several concerns that stem from the observation that their personal qualities have not been in the least considered, an offense all the more hurtful to the woman aware of the fact that in so close a relationship as marriage, and given the prerogatives that the laws in such matters accord the man, only respect for her as a person can ensure her an acceptable degree of protection. In the course of the negotiations in which I became involved, I saw quite clearly that the English show themselves to be a very naive nation when they determine people's worth according to their financial fortune, by asserting without reservation that a man is worth so many pounds. People of other nations do not say that; but that is precisely how they think, because that is how they act. I would not have been considered in the least if I had not had the many thousand thalers that made a union with me desirable. It really quite appeared as if man and woman were two opposed forces that only a third power could hold together.

Among all my suitors, I was most pleased with Herr von L——; but he was also the very one who conducted himself with the greatest caution. It was plain to see that he was able to bring into the bargaining, in addition to his not insignificant fortune, the venerable age of his family tree and that precisely this point posed the main difficulty. Prejudices of this kind take deep root if encouraged by some passion; yet precisely these same prejudices are abandoned with the greatest alacrity if one can replace the passion that nurtures them with another, destructive one; for people seek in all matters their own advantage and nothing but that. Since certificates of pedigree are never better preserved than in capsules of gold—no other metal can better protect such a rarity from gradual decay—

I believed I was not judging wrongly when I assumed that Herr von L—— could be more easily moved as soon as my fortune had been considerably augmented. Yet how was I to effect this augmentation? I pondered this question in vain until chance came to my aid.

I was enjoying myself one afternoon with one of my subordinate lovers when my aunt sent word that she wished to speak with me. I lost no time to hasten to her, for people whose heir one hopes to become lay greater claim to our attentions than any others once we are past the fickle years of youth. I found my aunt in her bed, though surely no weaker or feebler than I had otherwise encountered her. She told me she had drawn up her will and that I would be pleased with the final proof of her love for me; yet at the same time she asked me to stay some days with her, until her usual female companion, who had had to depart on a journey of great necessity, would return. I could in no way deny this request, as onerous as the task of caring for the ill was for me. The first four days I endured patiently; but since during this time my aunt's companion not only did not return but also wrote that her absence might last some months, I found that the interesting relationship in which I was then living gave me too much incentive to tear myself away from my aunt's sickbed.

In this situation the decisive question was how. I pondered the matter at length until it occurred to me that the legacy of my father had left me the most effective means. To shrink back in fear from such a thought I now, after having become so hardened and inured by fate, found impossible. I confess that this time I pondered with utmost cold-bloodedness how I would be able to control the situation in such a way that no suspicion could arise; and when I had straightened out that matter, I even grasped how I could carry out my plan so that the blame would fall upon the carelessness of others.

Accordingly, I hurried back home to place myself in possession of the means I most required. My aunt's maid was one of the many people of common status whom one can bring completely under control with a small gift. I assumed, upon my return to my aunt, an expression indicating that I felt the toil she was undertaking on behalf of her mistress deserved recognition from me as well, and with the gift I gave her I captured her affection for me even more than I had won her over with my benevolent kindness. As soon as I was thus sure of her devotion to me, I thought only of how I would carry out my plan. My aunt was receiving, since I had been at her side, all her medicine from me alone. It would have caused me—I do not deny it—no scruples at all to give her the lethal dose in place of the healing one myself; but I did not find that to be a very good idea. Feigning a severe headache, I withdrew at around the time she was due to take another dose, and I assigned her maid the task of giving her the medicine that was on her vanity table. Here I had placed the poison beside the medicine, but in such a way that no confusion of the two could work to the disadvantage of my intentions. And what I had expected did happen.

When I returned to my aunt's bedside, I found her already seized by convulsions. More boldly in control than when my husband died, I sent at once for a clergyman in order to provide her with the comfort she desired and of which, in this agonizing turn of events, she was so in need. I myself attempted to take his place until he arrived. What I said need not be repeated here. Suffice to say my aunt died after a few hours and a few days later was buried in most uplifting fashion, as I spared no expense that could have added to the splendor of her funeral.

My motives for this murder I have already indicated to you. Whether and how I justified it to myself—to explain that would lead too far afield; and now, after you have already come to know me so well, you can have no difficulty imagining the rationalizations with which I colored my actions, especially when you take into consideration the fact that my mental acuity had gained considerably as the result of my study of philosophy. A philosophy that concerns itself only with the transcendental must ultimately lead to sophistry; and in addition, among all my acquaintances and friends, males and females alike, I have known none who did not, once they had occupied themselves for some time with transcendental philosophy, go on to develop the most sophisticated egotism in all the world. To be sure, philosophers will be disinclined to see any causal connection here; yet it is all too clear to see if one delves more deeply than usual into people's characters.

My aunt's last testament made me wealthier by a considerable sum. When everything had been put in order and my treasure secured, I wanted to renew my acquaintance with Herr von L——. But I came too late; for a wealthy miss had already bested me in that race. I admit this irritated me more than a little, yet I soon calmed myself with the thought that my increased fortune assured me still greater freedom of choice among the men. I was reacting as all rich people do: my wealth was the measure of my worth and in this way increased my egotism to the point that I scorned all those who had nothing but their true merit.

All the more was I resolved to give my hand only to him who could ensure my further social advancement. Appearances began to mean everything to me, while my true being went totally to ruin. Not that I did not still place great value on certain pleasures, yet clearly these were something one could also come by outside of marriage. Quite separate in my judgment were husband and man, to the extent that I could not conceive of the former even in his most perfected form as in any way connected with the latter. I myself felt inclined to accept whatever was granted me.

While pursuing my plans in this manner, I continued my relationships with young men. The more of a novice one of them was, the more readily I welcomed him, and not merely for the sake of the greater pleasure he afforded, but mainly because I had him more in my power and as a result might fear less for my reputation. This reputation became more precious to me as the struggle that my actions were causing me to have with society became more acute. In this respect I was like a merchant who, when he is on the verge of bankruptcy, takes every measure possible to increase and secure his credit. Suppressing the selfishness to which I was actually thrall, I played the resigned and benevolent woman with such perfect deception that my old friends did not cease to sing my praises. By their assurances I was one of the most perfect women who had ever existed. Nor was there any virtue they did not ascribe to me, and they wanted but little to have declared my reason to have been of divine quality. Yet judgments of this kind deceive only those women who, as a rule, seldom know how things really stand and who can thus, in such matters, be tricked into believing whatever one wishes. Men arrive at their own private judgments; and since out of a kind of instinct they mistrust feminine virtues, all hymns of praise that women sing about such things simply waft past their ears unheeded, unless they themselves are witnesses to that virtue.

It was striking indeed that just when I was making my

greatest advances in the area of perversity, I found women prepared to extol my virtue with unequaled resolve. Not content with leading a life that was a mockery to all proper morality and, had it become known, would have earned me universal disdain, I also began now to misuse the trust and respect with which I had been credited, thanks to my status and my intelligence or impertinence, in order to commit acts of theft. You may be startled to read this confession. But why, after so many other confessions, should I keep this one a secret? Yes, I stole, and after always having committed theft successfully, I must confess I find it difficult to let pass an opportunity to steal again. How did I come to do this? As I did with all my other actions. With my ongoing need to forget myself, I had, by and by, to exhaust every possible act that cunning would allow. To theft I turned all the more quickly because the idea that one could not possess enough fortune in order to attain and ensure appearances and reputation had dominated my mind since the moment my hopes regarding Herr von L—— were dashed. A man, once he has fallen out with society, will rather rob than steal; on the other hand, a woman in that situation will rather steal than rob. This stems from the difference between the sexes. In my case, stealing was made easy by the fact that no one suspected me of being a thief. Without going into detail about it, I can tell you that I stole a great deal; but very seldom did anyone suspect me. Only twice did it happen that someone had doubts about my rectitude, and in both cases I was clever enough to ward off suspicion by voluntarily confessing and turning the entire unpleasant matter into a harmless jest. I confess that as I committed these despicable acts, nothing gave me more pleasure than noting how deluded people were about me. For just that reason I repeatedly put them to new tests, my precautions consisting, first, in the fact that just as magicians do, I never repeated my artful feats a second time with the same person and, second, in the fact that I never sold what I had got away with, convinced as I was that I would always have time to do so if by some special turn of fate I were to find it necessary to leave my fatherland and go abroad.

Since I frequently had too much cash and, as a woman, did not always find an opportunity to place it advantageously, I absolutely needed to find someone to act as an intermediary. The man to whom I turned was the son of a Jew with whom my father had conducted extensive business.

Moses S—— was, by his appearance, one of those mongrel types to be found in all large cities: the characteristic features of his Asiatic origins were, in his physiognomy, so blurred that one could have sworn he had not sprung from the seed of Israel. He himself seemed somehow to sense that fact; for he did and acted as a Christian, and if, late in life, he had been able to master his speech and pronunciation, people would generally have considered him to be a Christian. Yet what his exterior lacked in the way of Jewish features, his interior had in excess, and if people can call some Christians, on account of their greed, Jewish, then they would be perfectly well justified in calling this man the most Jewish Jew.

At first I employed him to supply me with mortgages, bonds, and other documents of financial security and investment; but since people of his type so gladly strive to further their good fortune, he too sought every opportunity to make himself indispensable to me. So, not content with keeping me supplied with documents of security, he made their purchase easier for me in every imaginable way by advancing me sums both large and small, as often as I had need of them, against no more than my signature. And not content with that, he supplied me with the most costly and fashionable goods at the most favorable prices possible. He assured me that his zeal in doing this sprang from the high esteem in which he held me personally and from the pleasant recollections of the good terms on which my father had stood with his. Of course, I was not so naive as not to understand his real meaning; yet I believed I could continue our association as long as it was advantageous to me. But this was exactly what the cunning Moses S—— intended.

An almost daily association does not fail to lead to a certain degree of familiarity between two parties, and whoever has dealt with Jews knows how adept they are at carrying this familiarity to its limit in the shortest possible time. Moses S—— may well have outdone all his brothers in this art. After barely three months I found him behaving towards me with a degree of liberty that lacked only a declaration of love to reach the limits of effrontery. As I had absolutely no idea of how I should confront such behavior without having to break off a very advantageous relationship, and as I felt with our every encounter that nothing is harder to resist than a determined show of impertinence, I resigned myself, in dealing with my banker, to my fate. With my offering absolutely no resistance, his declaration of love was not long in coming. I was ashamed of myself for the last time when his declaration came; but since I could not but laugh at the Jew's droll behavior, I made him still more bold. What more can I say? He won out over me.

From this moment on, Moses S—— believed he had complete power over me and was thus entitled to joint possession of all I owned, for there is scarcely a pretension he did not make upon me. If I wished not to let myself become the booty of a greedy Jew in the most laughable way in the world, I had to begin to be doubly on guard. The resistance with which I met several of his attempts to get the better of me served, by and by, to put him back in his place to some extent. But instead of giving up hope, he merely altered his manner of attack by playing up his magnanimity. Yet this mask was all too crude to serve him well in the long run; and since he saw clearly that he would never succeed in exploiting me, he resolved to give me up.

For some time I had been demanding unsuccessfully to settle my account with him; he put me off now with one excuse, now with another, of which none could be no more laughable coming from him than the notion that such a miserable matter as money could not be an issue between us. Then he finally brought me the record of my account, and while I must admit that it was correct as far as the individual items and entries were concerned, I could see that the actual sums had been falsified in the most hideous fashion. In particular the documents in my own handwriting listed sums quite different from the ones I had actually received, and one of them, on which an entry of fifty thaler had been changed to five hundred thaler, so clearly bore the signs of a forgery that I could have based a legal complaint on it. Now I saw very clearly what kind of person I was dealing with; but how was I to act in this thorny situation? Before I could gain time to ponder the matter, I yielded to the passion that we always feel when we discover we have been deceived or betrayed and that tells us quite clearly that we should always be honest.

"But Moses, how can you dare to attempt such changes with my handwriting?"

"Dear Madam," he responded, "I served you as an honest man; and if in doing so I have gained something, then, God knows, I worked hard to earn it." And this answer he kept repeating every time I cried out anew.

I could not make a legal complaint without ruining everything. And so as soon as I had to some degree come to think calmly about it, I told myself the best I could do was put a positive face on a bad situation and await my chance.

"You are quite right, Moses," I began, "and what I just said is to be taken as no more than jest. A minor detail should not come between us. Here is your money. We shall remain good friends." And with that I paid what he demanded and let him go his way, pleased with himself.

It is truly no easy matter to cheat a Jew who has cheated us. The more I was inclined to do so, the more insurmountable seemed the difficulties involved. To keep him from noticing my displeasure, I continued buying wares from him; I even purchased papers of investment from him as often as I required them. A half year may have passed when chance occasioned me to inquire about the state of my cash balance. I now believed I had found the means of bringing the wily Moses more than ever under my control.

Before I revealed to him what I had in mind, I gave him the strongest indications of my trust, not only by buying great quantities of articles from him, which I later, often at a loss, disposed of among my friends, but also by giving him great sums—secured by mortgages, of course—that he was to lend out at high interest as my broker. In this way I succeeded in making him forget what had happened between us. He himself gradually became the very picture of agreeability and might have been imagining that I had been seized by an irresistible passion for his esteemed self, when finally, in a confidential conversation that I had with him behind closed doors, I spoke of the possibility of opening and then closing cash pouches in such a way that there was no possibility of detecting an act of fraud. The interest of most Jews is mightily aroused as soon as someone explains to them how a federal crime can be committed without danger of detection. I had explained only half the plan when I saw an unusual fire kindled in Moses's eyes. The complete presentation of my plan he found enchanting. He was prepared at once to supply me with cash pouches. We tried the experiment, and it worked; and as we shared the proceeds, I could see that a connoisseur could find a delectable bird's nest soup from India no more to his liking than my Moses found the inner contents of the cash pouch. Once put back in circulation, the cash pouch, its deficit made up with copper and lead, went its way without the least repercussion. He would have been keen to try this trick even more often if I had shown more inclination to do so. We did repeat the experiment a few more times; but that was the end of it, since I considered the danger of getting caught too great and was using the deception as the means to another end.

For my intention was to put my Jew in such a position that if another such major coup—undertaken this time with an eye to revenge —were to succeed, he should never be tempted to speak of me. For this I had made all my preparations. Above all, my accounts with him were put in order and all my funds disbursed; he knew all about this himself, since everything had passed through his hands. Being then in possession of all necessary documents, I announced I was short of a considerable sum of cash that I had to have at once in order to satisfy the desires of a close relative. Moses was prepared to give me the money at once, since I promised I would not fail to show my gratitude for his help. In fact, when he brought me the money, I gave him a considerable gift for his efforts, and for the sum itself I gave him a bill of exchange in the same form as he was accustomed to receiving from me when we did business. This was all carried out amid the greatest friendliness between us, and he went his way without the least suspicion that a deception was afoot.

The bill of exchange had been written in corrosive ink. To make good my deception, I did not at once break off relationships with Moses, but no matter how much he attempted to carry on our business as before, I held back, except that I continued to take goods from him, which I paid for at once. If he called on me too often, I had him turned away. All was not as before; he noticed this himself and mentioned it, but he was unable to determine the exact cause and nature of the change.

At last my bill of exchange came due. How he may have felt when he opened it, he alone can know and say. Since he likely never encountered such a thing, he must have been taken aback without being able to explain what had happened. He was out of breath and deathly pale when he came into my room and handed me the note. I played the innocent, refusing to recognize the note as mine—which I could quite rightly do, since the handwriting was completely obscured and distorted—and promising to pay what was due as soon as he presented me with the one I had actually made out and signed. Moses exhibited the most unusual form of desperation that I have ever witnessed; but no matter what he might say or do, I held to the statement I had made and left it up to him to take me to court.

There was nothing he could do, for I was secretly pleased that everything had gone so well. He offered to accept payment at a considerable loss; but I would have none of that either, pointing out that I could then later be confronted with my note. At last our discussion had to come to an end. Moses departed from me with a bitter heart.

Whether he had managed to come out without taking a loss, I do not know, because I was no longer concerned about him; but there is no doubt he passed on to others the lovely invention I had discovered. This I know from his sudden departure from the capital city a year later. The experiment we had made with the cash pouches was repeated by others—but it failed. No sooner had the fraud been discovered than the authorities were on the trail of the perpetrators. The affair attracted more than a little attention, and I admit that as this was happening, my heart beat loudly. Fortunately for me, Moses was in even greater fear; for without delay he converted his entire fortune into paper, gave some pretense for taking a journey to Holland, and—never returned. Since the investigation—as far as I have been able to ascertain—made no mention of him, he had doubtless contented himself with teaching others the experiment without partaking of the profits bound up with it.

Now you will think that I had attained the pinnacle of depravity. Indeed, it would be difficult for a woman of twisted values—one who remains without any public influence on society and is thus incapable of organizing anything like the St. Bartholomew Massacre or the dragonades[30]—to achieve more than I did. Yet crimes can

[30] The reference to the St. Bartholomew Night Massacre and the dragonades concerns the infamous treatment of the Huguenots, first by Catherine de Medici, when she instigated the slaughter begun on 24 August 1572 (St. Bartholomew's Day), then by Louis XIV from 1681 to 1685, when dragoons were billeted with those Protestants and encouraged to mistreat their hosts. The implication is that the narrator's criminal acts pale in comparison with the grand-scale evil done by those in power.

be further combined and compounded; and so it came about that I exploited as a lover the same person whom I poisoned and robbed as an enemy.

In the very house in which I lived, a stranger had been lodging for some time of whom I took no notice until, at a loss for a new lover, I came into contact with him. By all physiognomical indications D——, as I shall call him, pursued a serious business, whatever it was; but his living habits, as far as I could deduce from certain signs, offered evidence that it was disreputable in nature. For very seldom did he arrive home before daybreak, then to sleep through the better part of the day—a daily routine that could scarcely escape my notice, since I lived directly below him.

In order to better inform myself about this man's life, I made a point of encountering him so often that he could not but take notice of me; and once we had made our mutual acquaintance, I made all those advances that give notice of a lively interest. It was not long before we had reached the level of intimacy I had intended. At this point, I learned that D—— was a professional gambler.

Acquisitive without being miserly, I expressed a desire to invest in part of his bank, and he willingly complied. I gave him a sum of one hundred pistoles, which he managed so well that within a time span of about two months I had regained my capital with interest.

D——, who imagined he had thus made me beholden

to him in a high degree and who, like almost all persons of his profession, wished to extend his adventurous ways beyond the bounds of the gaming table, let fall a variety of signals intended to show very clearly that he was not at all averse to entering into a closer relationship with me. I for my part had to treat the matter with delicacy if I wanted to avoid the trap I had laid for myself; for you may be sure I had not dreamt of entering into a serious relationship with a professional gambler.

At the start I acted as if I did not understand him; and when he explained his intentions to me, I played the conscientious one and demanded that he return my capital. But this was all the less to his liking, since, in his efforts to win my trust, he had sacrificed all his own winnings and perhaps even a bit more. In order to ease my conscience, he pointed out to me that fortune was fickle and that he could not guarantee I would not lose my winnings.

It was a strange struggle now between us; for precisely what he wanted to use to tie me more closely to him was for me the motive for breaking off with him, by which I mean the winnings that I had already made and that I wished to keep.

D—— was much more subtle than I had assumed. In order to keep the money I had already entrusted to him and in order, if possible, to come into possession of my entire fortune, he began to appeal to my weaker side, namely by instigating all manner of rumors at my expense to circulate in the capital city, the least of which would suffice to ruin my reputation irretrievably.

I confess I was actually on the verge of yielding. Yet in order not to be overly hasty, I returned to the social circles of my old friends, whom I could look upon as the surest gauge of my reputation; and the fact that I was accorded the same reception I had always received among them was enough to expose D——, in my eyes, as a liar.

Giving him the least indication of this would have greatly aggravated my situation, and so I continued with him as before, not repeating my demand and waiting for the right opportunity; in fact, I even doubled the capital I had entrusted to him. He, in order to give me no less proof of his trust in me, asked me if I would take his cash holdings into my care, since they were not very safe in his rooms when he was away from the house.

That was all I could have desired. Doubling my show of friendliness, I gave him the most definite reasons to hope, except that I was only postponing the goal of his desires to a somewhat later point in time. And with this serving to increase his trust in me, I seized the occasion when he fell ill with a fever to treat him with a medicine that made any recovery impossible. His cash purse, which he had left with me even during his illness, remained in my possession after his death. What it contained I appropriated with a calm conscience, telling myself that it was, at least in part, the earnings of my fortune and that D——'s relatives, if he had any, would never lay eyes on any of it, since it would first have to go through many pairs of hands that were not especially known for their cleanliness. I most likely would not have treated poor D—— in such a manner if I had known any other means of dealing with him without causing a scandal. Since at one point he had looked upon me as his prize and prey, I had to believe that if I wanted to break with him, he would take a revenge that could have cost me my reputation; for people of his type know nothing of the delicate consideration with which our sex wishes to be treated; none of their training extends beyond a certain courteousness they show their punters and fellow players. I confess that the relationship with him made me feel my worst ever in every respect.

I now began to realize that for me there could be no standing still on the path upon which I had embarked. Great was the depression I felt whenever I thought about my life; still greater was my depression at the fact that I could not reach my goal by any means. The decline of my charms, which I was struggling to halt, increased with each day, with the enlargement of my pores—the result of a lascivious life—imparting to my face an ugliness that bordered on the disgusting and that resisted all artful means of improving my color. The attractiveness of my fortune was not so great that, acting in isolation, it would have persuaded the kind of man I wished to possess to ignore all other things, particularly as I approached the matter in a purely business-like way and was absolutely bent upon gaining, be it in terms of status or of fortune, just as much from the relationship as I brought to it. Of every ten men with whom I began negotiations, eight would withdraw at once; and if the others lingered on, it could be due only to a lack of moral tact, as a result of which they remained briefly in doubt as to whether it was still worth considering a relationship with me. One insult followed another, with their all combining to cause a bitterness that could scarcely have been greater.

In this situation I was quite averse to remaining in the capital. But where was I to turn to feel better? In any case I felt that a second trip to the spa would give me some ease, and so I went. The world I entered was a new one, and at the outset it seemed as if I could take up new habits in this new world. Here there was not the least call for hypocrisy; here I could give up my plans to conquer and gain; here I was allowed to set upon my acquisitiveness all those limits that society holds so important to observe; here I had no need to fear any of those collisions that had made me a poisoner; in short, if a conversion was possible, it was possible here. How ardently I desired such a change! Yet the color a character has once assumed can no more be completely washed out than can the dye applied to a fabric; elimination and destruction are the only means. Thus my needs tormented me in the new relationships that I entered into, and my passion was all the more raging, the more difficulties I had to overcome in order to satisfy it. If I held to my lascivious ways, it was only because that path promised the least danger; for I know only too well how hard it was for me to fight my acquisitiveness and to withstand the bitterness I felt towards various of my female rivals. The deity itself would have had to refashion me; it was not within my power.

Struggling with such depressing feelings, I believed I could ease them by continuing my travels. Yet now things no longer made the impression on me that, on my previous journey, I had to thank for some diversion. The desire to make new acquaintances I had lost since I had come to feel constantly so ashamed of myself, in part physically, in part morally. No matter where I stayed, I was plagued by boredom. Now the time had come to direct my weapons at myself. More than once I was on the verge of doing so; but love of life has not yet died out where there still prevails a need whose satisfaction is bound up with pleasure. Thus as unpleasant as I had found residence in the capital, I nevertheless returned to it soon. I had imagined I would find it possible to live in solitude; yet all too acutely did I learn the opposite. Persons of my type, I believe, can make solitude bearable only through ardent piety; yet I was incapable of such piety, because all my ideas about human nature made me more inclined to freethinking than to faith.

After my return to the capital I resumed my old way of life as best I could. Yet it seemed as if in my early years I had had too much success to have even the least success now. I relented in my pretensions by lowering my expectations, but the results remained the same: even court councillors and military attachés rejected me. What didn't I do to convince myself that I was not yet so totally forsaken, so totally rejected! Through some old women whom I was still keeping in my service, I had men whose names I barely knew invited to me as to a certain lady who was desirous of their company. While this strange manner of procuration succeeded on some occasions, it more often did not, and not seldom would a man turn away at my doorstep upon seeing my name below the bell. There is likely no ploy I did not use to ensure myself, if not pleasure, then at least diversion. Without my own admission, this would not seem believable; and yet I must not allow myself to go into detail if I wish not to lose credibility. Suffice to say in general: the greater my bitterness grew, the more daring did I become with my machinations. I conspired against great families, and it is truly no fault of mine that they were not destroyed, root and branch. Whenever I saw fortunate people, my blood would boil at once. Most sensitive was my aversion to the sight of unbound gaiety; and had it been in my power to banish such a sight from the earth, I would have done so with pleasure. If there was still any pleasure for me at all, then it was in reading French memoirs from the times of Henry II and his wife, the infamous Catherine de Medici; for in them I found characters of my own type.[31] With what rapturous feelings would I have been filled by the outbreak of a revolution right in my midst!

You will not be able to grasp how I concealed such a life from those around me. Whether I was completely successful in doing so I cannot claim for certain; yet in this regard I took precautions that more or less had to achieve their ends. First, I never kept as many servants as my status required and as my fortune allowed; a chambermaid and one male servant sufficed, and I conscientiously saw to it that the latter was a married man and did not sleep under my roof. One of the advantages of that arrangement was that no close degree of confiding could develop between the two. Second, I treated my people with as much strictness on the one hand as benevolence on the other. I always spoke very little with them; but I

[31] The Italian-born Catherine de Medici (1519–89) became the wife of Duke Henry of Orleans, the future Henry II of France, in 1533 and thus, in 1547, when her mentor King Francis I died, the queen of France. She survived the resentment that the French populace felt toward an Italian queen and the rivalry for her husband's attention with Diane Poitiers, as well as the religious wars involving the Huguenots, to preserve the monarchy and provide the French with three kings: Francis II, Charles IX, and Henry III. While her power was limited during the reign of Henry II and of her son Francis II, she emerged as a political power during the reign of Charles IX from 1560 to 1574, during which time she instigated the St. Bartholomew Night Massacre of the Huguenots in 1572.

let them lack for nothing, and by paying them very well I made them inclined to fulfil my every wish and even to respect as holy decree what I might offer them in the way of some very unusual task. Third, I never had them act as my mediators for any of my plans, whatever their nature; for that, as you will recall, I had other people to do my bidding. Fourth, I would dismiss them without compunction as soon as I had the least suspicion that I had fallen in their esteem; but in doing so I never failed to give them, shortly before their departure, a gift, whereby I bribed them anew on my behalf. Barely a few of them knew what had caused their dismissal, and they were thus more or less compelled to ascribe it to a whim. Several of them would offer me their services again after some time. But in such cases there is no lack of apologies; and since I was well aware of the reasons for which I had dismissed them, I never let myself be persuaded into taking them on again.— Unfortunately, this treatment was necessary if I wanted to continue playing my role in society. The least deviation from it would have been the most unforgivable weakness I could have allowed. You yourself know the positive light in which women still hold me. Can anyone be more despicable and more popular than I?

But enough, and enough again. You see from these confessions how I have become what I am. I have passed in silence over nothing essential, and far less have I glossed over anything. Pass upon me now your judgment of damnation or pity me—as you wish. It is all the same to me; for I shall no longer exist when these confessions come into your possession.

If you believe I am tortured by regret, then you are wrong. Upon a life like mine one cannot look back with pleasure; but to feel regret about it is just as impossible. Tell me yourself what I should regret. Was it not all a closely knit chain of causes and effects in which the last is always the cause of new? Here there was absolutely no beginning and no end; so here the first look into the past could not but cause confusion.

Perhaps I shall not end as I think I shall; but even if my crimes become known and the justice system calls me to account, I shall never for a moment condemn myself. I have thought too long about myself to fall victim to a moment of weakness. They can condemn me; they can even destroy me; but they cannot convict or punish me. I am absolutely beyond all punishment, because what I have done was always necessary, given my individuality and given the circumstances. The difference between compulsion and obligation has always been, according to my inmost conviction, a scholastic fine point. Since reason itself is something acquired, it can initiate no new sequence of actions but rather only compete in accordance with its inner force. In a word: freedom of will I find not at all a matter of doubt; I am most firmly convinced of its absence.

But even if I do not fall into the hands of the justice system, my future remains lamentable in the extreme—so lamentable, in fact, that I am uncertain whether I would not rather die at the hands of the hangman than keep on living. As long as I continue to breathe, my life is, in one way or another, the ruin of others. I am like the poison tree that creates around itself a vast desolation. My mental fevers are much too strong to be confused, and as long as they continue in my service, there is nothing to expect of me but evil. I must be destroyed if there is to be any peace. Only in that way can I myself be brought to peace.

As things now stand, I see nothing before me but abyss upon abyss; but do not imagine I am frightened by that! It is my only remaining pleasure to see them open before me and to plunge into none of them. Yet should someday come the time when this plunge cannot be avoided, I shall accept my fate with all possible resignation and consider it good fortune that my spirit dies with me and does not, as my father's did, live on, evolving, in another being.

Make my confessions known in the form in which I have given them to you. Weak souls, of course, will find outrageous the fact that I have written them down with such audacity; but on that point I think differently. In the first place they contain the truth and therewith insights about human nature that are by no means trivial. In the second place it is up to the readers to turn them to a good purpose. You ask, to what purpose? Nothing is more neglected in our times than the upbringing and education of our daughters. I am a warning example of an education that was more masculine than feminine; and although I do not clearly understand how the former could have been avoided in my case, that does not mean it could not be avoided in general. If people do not use my example to keep young girls within the bounds of femininity, then I predict that many will have need only of the right circumstances to follow in my footsteps. The greatest legacy I can leave the world is the urgent call for the better education of young girls; for dependent upon that are the fortunes of marriage, and upon that the fortunes of the world. And what could better support this call than confessions like mine?— To continue:

The model I offer will someday go to ruin; but that it not recur can be guaranteed only if the structure of society attains greater completeness. How this greater completeness is to be brought about—that I do not know, and even if I did, I would not enter into a discussion about it, because the manifold crimes that still at present burden society would hardly come to an end. I want to point out only one thing, because it is most closely tied to my transgressions. Cunning can be vanquished only by fear. And so an end to crimes born of cunning can happen only if that part of our public administration that we call the police is far more fully developed. How could I have gone about poisoning so audaciously if there were public autopsies, by which I mean an inquest carried out by expert men whose main concern would be none other than to ascertain the natural or unnatural cause of a death? Such inquests are necessary in every capital city, because wherever a great concentration of people brings increased friction, crimes of all kinds are unavoidable. There were once inquests. But because they became an object of idle curiosity, an end was put to them. Yet they should have been improved. As far as I know human beings, they can be brought to do good only out of fear. What would become of all society if this fear were suspended for only a few days? Since the social situation has become simply an artificial one, governments must never rest; their most gentle demand must be strong enough when it comes to preventing the repetition of a misdeed. To destroy by punishing is a minor matter; justice will always do its duty if it must assert itself. But to forestall the need to punish is a far more artful task, and the police must perform it.

Once a major crime has been committed, then, I repeat once again, there can be no end; human nature does not tolerate it. Madame de Brinvilliers poisoned one hundred and fifty people in a span of ten years.[32] How often

[32] The marquise de Brinvilliers (1630–76) was born Marie Madeleine d'Aubray. The conflict with her father resulting from her affair with one Sainte-Croix led her to conspire, with Sainte-Croix and the

I thought of her and how well I understand this monster upon whom others look with astonishment. Surely a person can reach the point of playing with poison, just as there have often been princes for whom the state of peace was unbearable and who for just that reason and without pangs of conscience sent their subjects to be slaughtered by the thousands. But even discounting such frivolousness, people are compelled by the very nature of a crime to repeat it. The situation is much the same as when one comes into financial difficulties. Once one has gone into debt and is then pressed by the demands of ruthless creditors to produce the money at any cost, one soon reaches the point of merely covering one debt by incurring another; and as the problem becomes worse, it cannot but reach the point where a person succumbs to the progressively growing weight of debt. Thus the important thing above all is that the first steps are made difficult, and this can be done no more effectively than by measures that prohibit such crimes and by educating people about these measures. Such prohibition is a great science that does not yet exist but that the coming fifty years will bring about.

How much I could still tell you if I did not have to believe that you have lost the patience to hear any more.

---

notorious Italian poisoner Exili, to poison her enemies, this after testing her concoctions in various hospitals. Her many poisonings and attempted poisonings came to light after Sainte-Croix's death, and she was eventually tried and executed.

At the start of my confessions I told you, "As to Him who judges all the world, so to you I want to reveal my inmost self." I have kept my word and thus paid your virtue the greatest homage I could offer. Farewell; and whatever you might hear about me after my death, believe it only insofar as it agrees with these confessions.

Works Cited in the Notes

Grimm, Jacob, and Wilhelm Grimm. *Deutsches Wörterbuch*. Vol. 11, sec. 1, pt. 2. Leipzig: Hirzel, 1952. Print.

Mozart, Wolfgang Amadeus. *The Magic Flute: Translated from German and Including Musical Highlight Transcriptions*. Libretto by Emanuel Schikaneder. Ed. Burton D. Fisher. Bilingual ed. Coral Gables: Opera Journeys, 2001. Print.

Shakespeare, William. *The Complete Works of William Shakespeare*. Ed. W. G. Clark and W. Aldis Wright. 2 vols. New York: Doubleday, 1965. Print.

———. *Hamlet: Prinz von Dänemark*. 1798. Trans. A[ugust] W[ilhelm] von Schlegel. Ed. Levin Schücking. Berlin: Tempel, 1950. Print.

Wieland, Christoph Martin. "Rechtfertigung der berühmten Frau von Maintenon gegen eine höchst ungerechte Anklage: Gezogen aus einem durch die berüchtigten Bekenntnisse einer Giftmischerin veranlaßten zufälligen Gespräche." Ed. Bernhard Seuffert. *Zeitschrift für Bücherfreunde* 4.2 (1913): 308–14. Print.

Modern Language Association of America Texts and Translations

Texts

Anna Banti. *"La signorina" e altri racconti*. Ed. and introd. Carol Lazzaro-Weis. 2001.

Bekenntnisse einer Giftmischerin, von ihr selbst geschrieben. Ed. and introd. Raleigh Whitinger and Diana Spokiene. 2009.

Adolphe Belot. *Mademoiselle Giraud, ma femme*. Ed and introd. Christopher Rivers. 2002.

Dovid Bergelson. אָפּגאַנג. Ed. and introd. Joseph Sherman. 1999.

Elsa Bernstein. *Dämmerung: Schauspiel in fünf Akten*. Ed. and introd. Susanne Kord. 2003.

Edith Bruck. *Lettera alla madre*. Ed. and introd. Gabriella Romani. 2006.

Isabelle de Charrière. *Lettres de Mistriss Henley publiées par son amie*. Ed. Joan Hinde Stewart and Philip Stewart. 1993.

Isabelle de Charrière. *Trois femmes: Nouvelle de l'Abbé de la Tour*. Ed. and introd. Emma Rooksby. 2007.

François-Timoléon de Choisy, Marie-Jeanne L'Héritier, and Charles Perrault. *Histoire de la Marquise-Marquis de Banneville*. Ed. Joan DeJean. 2004.

Sophie Cottin. *Claire d'Albe*. Ed. and introd. Margaret Cohen. 2002.

Marceline Desbordes-Valmore. *Sarah*. Ed. Deborah Jenson and Doris Y. Kadish. 2008.

Claire de Duras. *Ourika*. Ed. Joan DeJean. Introd. DeJean and Margaret Waller. 1994.

Şeyh Galip. *Hüsn ü Aşk*. Ed. and introd. Victoria Rowe Holbrook. 2005.

Françoise de Graffigny. *Lettres d'une Péruvienne*. Introd. Joan DeJean and Nancy K. Miller. 1993.

Sofya Kovalevskaya. Нигилистка. Ed. and introd. Natasha Kolchevska. 2001.

Thérèse Kuoh-Moukoury. *Rencontres essentielles*. Introd. Cheryl Toman. 2002.

Juan José Millás. *"Trastornos de carácter" y otros cuentos*. Introd. Pepa Anastasio. 2007.

Emilia Pardo Bazán. *"El encaje roto" y otros cuentos*. Ed. and introd. Joyce Tolliver. 1996.

Rachilde. *Monsieur Vénus: Roman matérialiste*. Ed. and introd. Melanie Hawthorne and Liz Constable. 2004.

Marie Riccoboni. *Histoire d'Ernestine*. Ed. Joan Hinde Stewart and Philip Stewart. 1998.

Eleonore Thon. *Adelheit von Rastenberg*. Ed. and introd. Karin A. Wurst. 1996.

Translations

Anna Banti. *"The Signorina" and Other Stories*. Trans. Martha King and Carol Lazzaro-Weis. 2001.

Adolphe Belot. *Mademoiselle Giraud, My Wife*. Trans. Christopher Rivers. 2002.

Dovid Bergelson. *Descent*. Trans. Joseph Sherman. 1999.

Elsa Bernstein. *Twilight: A Drama in Five Acts*. Trans. Susanne Kord. 2003.

Edith Bruck. *Letter to My Mother*. Trans. Brenda Webster with Gabriella Romani. 2006.

Isabelle de Charrière. *Letters of Mistress Henley Published by Her Friend*. Trans. Philip Stewart and Jean Vaché. 1993.

Isabelle de Charrière. *Three Women: A Novel by the Abbé de la Tour*. Trans. Emma Rooksby. 2007.

François-Timoléon de Choisy, Marie-Jeanne L'Héritier, and Charles Perrault. *The Story of the Marquise-Marquis de Banneville*. Trans. Steven Rendall. 2004.

Confessions of a Poisoner, Written by Herself. Trans. Raleigh Whitinger and Diana Spokiene. 2009.

Sophie Cottin. *Claire d'Albe*. Trans. Margaret Cohen. 2002.

Marceline Desbordes-Valmore. *Sarah*. Trans. Deborah Jenson and Doris Y. Kadish. 2008.

Claire de Duras. *Ourika*. Trans. John Fowles. 1994.

Şeyh Galip. *Beauty and Love*. Trans. Victoria Rowe Holbrook. 2005.

Françoise de Graffigny. *Letters from a Peruvian Woman*. Trans. David Kornacker. 1993.

Sofya Kovalevskaya. *Nihilist Girl*. Trans. Natasha Kolchevska with Mary Zirin. 2001.

Thérèse Kuoh-Moukoury. *Essential Encounters*. Trans. Cheryl Toman. 2002.

Juan José Millás. *"Personality Disorders" and Other Stories*. Trans. Gregory B. Kaplan. 2007.

Emilia Pardo Bazán. *"Torn Lace" and Other Stories*. Trans. María Cristina Urruela. 1996.

Rachilde. *Monsieur Vénus: A Materialist Novel*. Trans. Melanie Hawthorne. 2004.

Marie Riccoboni. *The Story of Ernestine*. Trans. Joan Hinde Stewart and Philip Stewart. 1998.

Eleonore Thon. *Adelheit von Rastenberg*. Trans. George F. Peters. 1996.

Texts and Translations in One-Volume Anthologies

Modern Italian Poetry. Ed. and trans. Ned Condini. Introd. Dana Renga. 2009.

Modern Urdu Poetry. Ed., introd., and trans. M. A. R. Habib. 2003.

Nineteenth-Century Women's Poetry from France. Ed. Gretchen Schultz. Trans. Anne Atik, Michael Bishop, Mary Ann Caws, Melanie Hawthorne, Rosemary Lloyd, J. S. A. Lowe, Laurence Porter, Christopher Rivers, Schultz, Patricia Terry, and Rosanna Warren. 2008.

Nineteenth-Century Women's Poetry from Spain. Ed. Anna-Marie Aldaz. Introd. Susan Kirkpatrick. Trans. Aldaz and W. Robert Walker. 2008.

Spanish American Modernismo. Ed. Kelly Washbourne. Trans. Washbourne with Sergio Waisman. 2007.